THE DEMON BREED

THE DEMON BREED

JAMES H. SCHMITZ

ACE BOOKS, INC.
1120 Avenue of the Americas
New York, N.Y. 10036

DEDICATION:
Here's a book for Betty Mae——

THE DEMON BREED

1

As THE PAIN haze began to thin out, Ticos Cay was somewhat surprised to find he was still on his feet. This had been a brutally heavy treatment—at moments it had seemed almost impossible to control. However, he *had* controlled it. The white-hot sensations, which hadn't quite broken through with full impact into consciousness, faded to something like a sullenly lingering glow. Then that faded too. His vision began to clear.

Cautiously he allowed himself to accept complete awareness of his body again. It was still an unpleasant experience. There were sharp twinges everywhere, a feeling of having been recently pierced and sliced by tiny hot knives; the residue of pain. The lasting damage caused by one of these pain treatments to the human nervous system and sensory apparatus was slight but measurable. The accumulative effect of a series of treatments was no longer slight; and there had been over twenty of them during the past weeks. Each time now, taking stock of the physical loss he had suffered during the process, Ticos wondered whether he would be forced to acknowledge that the damage had spread to the point where it could no longer be repaired.

However, it hadn't happened on this occasion. His mind was fogged over; but it always was for a short while after a treatment. Reassured, he shifted attention from his internal condition to his surroundings.

The big room had come back into focus. Most of it was

dark because the demons had cut out all but a central section of the ceiling illumination. There remained a pool of light which enclosed most of the long worktable against which he leaned and the raised platform twenty feet away, from which they were watching him. The shelves and walls beyond, the rows of biological specimens, the arrays of analyzing and recording equipment, were in darkness.

Ticos Cay looked about, taking it in, drawing the trappings of reality back around him. He looked last at the demons.

"You succeeded again in avoiding the feeling of pain?" asked the small one of the three.

Ticos considered. The identity of the small demon was still blurred but coming clear. Yes, his name was Koll . . . the Great Palach Koll. One of the most influential among the leaders of the Everliving. Second in command of the Voice of Action. . . .

Ticos admonished himself: *Be very careful of Koll!*

He made a sound between what might have been a muttering attempt to speak and a groan. He could have replied immediately. But it wouldn't do to think foggily while being interrogated—and particularly not while being interrogated by Koll.

The three stared silently, unmoving. Their skins, harnesses and other equipment gleamed wetly as if they had come out of the sea only minutes before entering the room. Which might be the case; salt water was the demons' element, and they became sick and uncomfortable if they remained too long away from it. The one to the right of Koll held a device with a glowing blue eye. When the glow brightened, a pain treatment was about to begin. The one at the left of Koll had a weapon trained on Ticos. These two were squat heavy creatures hunkering on muscular hopping legs. Ticos had been obliged to watch one of their kind wrap his arms around the rib cage of a man and crush the man slowly to death without apparent effort.

It had been done at Koll's direction. The big demons were underlings; they were called Oganoon by the Palachs. Koll was of the same species but not large or heavy. Like many of the Great Palachs, he was a wrinkled miniature, not much more than a foot high. Cloaked and hooded, he looked like a shrunken mummy. But he could move like springing steel. Ticos had seen Koll leap eight feet to plunge a paralyzing needle into the eye of an Oganoon who had angered him. He struck five or six times, so quickly that the victim seemed to stiffen in death without understanding what had occurred.

Ticos strongly preferred not to anger Koll. But he needed as long a period of silence as Koll would permit to clear his head for the questions that would be directed at him. He had been maintaining a precarious balance between considerations on that order for some time. He waited until the speaking slit above Koll's eyes writhed open, then said unsteadily, "I could not avoid all the pain. But it remained tolerable."

"It remained tolerable!" the speaking slit repeated as if Koll were musing over the statement. Ticos was accustomed to the fact that many of the Everliving had an excellent command of human speech, but Koll's voice still seemed unnatural to him. It was a deep warm voice, rich and strong, which shouldn't be issuing from such a malevolent little entity. "These children are afraid of you, Dr. Cay," it told him. "Did you know that?"

"No, I didn't," Ticos said.

11

"At a tenth of the setting used here," Koll explained, "these instruments are employed to punish them for serious offenses. They are in terror of them. They are afraid of you because you seem able to bear agony beyond their comprehension. And there are other reasons. . . . Your communicator has recorded six call signals during the past two days."

Ticos nodded. "So I heard."

"You predicted that one of the so-called Tuvelas would attempt to contact you here."

Ticos hesitated, said, "The term Tuvela is yours. The person to whom you refer is known to me as a Guardian."

"Apparently the same class of creature," said Koll. "A creature assumed by some to possess abnormal qualities. Among them the quality of being invincible. Dr. Cay, what do you know of these remarkable qualities—if they exist?"

Ticos shrugged. "As I've told you, I've known of the Guardians and of their function in our civilization for a relatively short time. They operate very secretly. I've had personal contacts with only one of them. She appears to me to be an exceptionally capable human being. But if she or the Guardians generally have abnormal qualities, I don't know of them." He added, "Evidently the Ever-living know more about the Guardians than I do."

"That is possible. You said they claim to be immortal."

Ticos shook his head. "I was told they've developed methods of restoring youthful health to an organism and maintaining it for a long period. I was not told they were immortal. To me the word does not have significant meaning."

"The concept of immortal entities is meaningless to you, Dr. Cay?"

Ticos hesitated again because this could become dangerous ground in speaking to a Palach. But he said, "Who can
prove he is immortal before he's reached the end of time?"

Koll's dark face twitched. He might have been amused.
"Who indeed?" he agreed. "Describe to me your relationship with these Guardians."

Ticos had described that relationship to Koll several times
before. He said, "Two years ago I was asked whether I
would enter their service. I accepted."

"Why?"

"I'm aging, Great Palach. Among my rewards was to
be instruction in the Guardian's methods of obtaining longevity and regaining the advantages of youth."

"They've given you such instructions?"

"I've been instructed in some of the fundamental approaches. My progress evidently is satisfactory."

"In what way do you serve them, Dr. Cay?"

"I'm still undergoing a training process and haven't been
told what my service is to be. I assume that my scientific
background will play a part in it."

"The nerve controls you practice to distort the effects of
the pain-giver were acquired through the longevity exercises?"

"Yes, they were."

A long pause followed his reply. Koll's speaking slit had
closed and he remained unmoving. The lower sections of
his double-lensed eyes were lidded; the upper sections
stared with a kind of baleful blankness at Ticos. The hulking
servitors had become equally immobile, probably as a sign
of respect. Ticos wasn't sure what the pause meant. The
same thing had occurred during earlier interrogations. Perhaps the tiny monster was simply reflecting on what had

13

been said. But he appeared sunk in a remote trance. If he was addressed now he would ignore it, and he seemed unaware of motion about him. Ticos suspected there was the equivalent of human insanity in Koll. Even Great Palachs of his own rank seemed afraid of him, and he treated them with barely veiled contempt. His dark cowl and cloak were of utilitarian material and often indifferently clean, while they concealed their dwarfish bodies under richly ornamented garments, gleaming with jewels. Apparently they preferred to avoid Koll's company; but his influence on them was very strong.

The speaking slit above the eyes twisted open again.

"Dr. Cay," Koll's voice said, "I become increasingly inclined to add you to my museum of humanity. You have seen my collection?"

Ticos cleared his throat. "Yes," he said.

"Of course you have," Koll said, as if the fact had just occurred to him. "I showed it to you. As a warning not to lie to us. In particular, not to lie to me."

Ticos said warily, "I have been quite careful not to lie to you, Great Palach."

"Have you? I'm not at all certain of it," said Koll. "Do you believe that the person who is attempting to reach you by communicator is the Guardian of whom you told us?"

Ticos nodded. "Yes. The Guardian Etland."

"Why should it be she?"

"No one else has the call symbol of my communicator."

"Because you were to remain isolated here?"

"Yes."

"The Guardian Etland supervises your training?"

"Yes."

"You describe her as a young female," said Koll.

"I said she appears young," Ticos corrected him. "I don't know her age."

"You say that these Guardians or Tuvelas have developed a form of longevity which provides even the appearance of their species' youth. . . ."

"The Guardian Etland has implied that."

"And yet," said Koll, "you tell us the Guardians assigned you the task of searching here for substances among the life forms of this world which promote longevity. What interest could the Guardians have in research which yields them no more than they possess?"

Ticos shrugged. "I know they're testing me in various ways, and it may be that this is their manner of testing my ability as a biochemist. But it's also possible that they're still interested in finding simpler or more dependable methods of gaining longevity than their present ones."

"What part does the use of chemicals play in their present methods?"

"I don't know. I've described the basic approaches I was told to practice. I've been given no hint of the nature of more advanced longevity procedures. My research is confined to the observation of effects in my test material."

"You've suggested that research at this level could be of value to the Everliving. . . ."

"I haven't suggested it," Ticos said. "I realize, of course, that a number of Palachs observe my test results and analyze the substances involved."

"Don't let yourself assume their scientific interest assures your continuing safety, Dr. Cay. Our methods of obtaining individual longevity require no improvement. I'm certain you are lying to us. I intend to determine in what manner you are lying. Why did you request permission to respond to the Guardian's call?"

"I explained my purpose to the Palach Moga," Ticos said.

"Explain it to me."

Ticos indicated the equipment and specimens in the darkened recesses of the room. "This project is the Guardian Etland's responsibility. I and my training are her responsibility. Until your arrival she came here at very regular intervals to inspect the progress I made. Since then she hasn't come here."

"What do you deduce from that?"

"It's possible that the Guardians know of your presence."

"I don't consider that a possibility, Dr. Cay."

Ticos shrugged. "It's the only explanation I see for the Guardian Etland's failure to maintain her schedule. The Guardians may prefer you to leave quietly before there is a general disturbance. If I'm permitted to turn on the communicator when she signals again, we may learn that the Guardian is on her way here to speak to the Everliving rather than to me. . . ."

"She would come knowingly into the area we hold?" said Koll.

"From what several Palachs have told me," Ticos remarked, "it would not be surprising conduct in a Tuvela. If it is true—"

"We'll assume it isn't true, Dr. Cay."

"Then," said Ticos, "I should still be permitted to take the call and attempt to divert her from visiting me at this time. If she does not know you are here and arrives, she will discover you are here. And even if you are able to prevent her from leaving again—"

Koll made a hissing sound. "If we are able to prevent her from leaving?"

"Your own records, as you've implied to me, indicate that Tuvelas are extremely resourceful beings," Ticos observed mildly. "But if you should capture or kill the Guardian, others will come promptly in search of her. Eventually your presence must be revealed." He shrugged. "I don't want these things to happen. As a servant of the Guardians, it is my duty to prevent them from happening if I can. As you're aware, I've been attempting to persuade some of the Everliving that your plans against my species must be abandoned before a general conflict becomes inevitable."

"I know that," said Koll. "You've had an astonishing—and shameful—degree of success. The Voice of Caution becomes increasingly insistent. Even the suggested use of your communicator is supported. Is it possible, Dr. Cay, that you are a Guardian who allowed himself to be captured in order to confuse the Everliving and weaken their resolution?"

"No," Ticos said. "I'm not a Guardian."

"You're a Hulon?"

"Since that's the name you give the general run of humanity, yes, I'm a Hulon."

"It was the name we had for a vicious and stupid creature we encountered in our past," Koll remarked. "We destroyed the creature, so the name was free to be bestowed again. Despite your efforts, our plans won't be abandoned, Dr. Cay. I know you're lying. Not too clumsily, but it will not be long before we put your story to the test. . . . Now attend to your collection here—and reflect occasionally on mine. . . ."

Ticos did not see him make any gesture, but the Oga-

17

noon on Koll's right snapped the nerve-torture instrument to one of the harness straps about its bulky body and half turned. The tiny cowled mummy made one of its startlingly quick leaps and was perched on the underling's shoulder. The group moved off the platform and along a raised walkway toward the exit door, the armed servitor bringing up the rear, backing off in short powerful hops, weapon still pointed alertly at Ticos Cay. The lighting brightened back to normal in the big room.

Ticos watched the three vanish through the door, heard the heavy click of its locks. He drew a somewhat shaky breath, picked up a boxed device from the worktable and fastened it by its strap to his belt. It was a complicated instrument through which he controlled temperature, humidity, radiation absorption levels and various other matters connected with his biological specimens in different sections of the room.

His hands were unsteady. The interrogation hadn't gone to his liking. Koll wasn't his usual savagely menacing self—and that in spite of some deliberate provocation. He'd made use of the pain-giver only once. Koll, for Koll, had been affable.

It seemed a bad sign. It indicated that Koll was as confident as he appeared to be that he could dispel the doubts Ticos was nourishing in other leading Palachs by proving their prisoner had misinformed them. And, as a matter of fact, Ticos had totally misinformed them. Over a course of weeks he'd created a carefully organized structure of lies, half-truths and disturbing insinuations designed to fill the Everliving with the fear of Man, or at any rate with the fear of Tuvelas. Who, as far as Ticos Cay knew, didn't exist. Sometimes he'd been hard put to remain consistent, but by now the pattern was so familiar that it held an occasional illusion of truth even for him.

It had been effective in restricting their plans until now. In spite of Koll, it might remain effective—but that depended on a large factor of chance. Ticos sighed inaudibly. He'd reduced the factor as much as possible, but it was still too large. Far too large!

He moved slowly about the room, manipulating the studs of his device now and then, tending to the needs of the biological specimens. He'd never been able to determine whether he was under visual observation or not, but it was possible, and he must not appear too concerned. Occasionally he felt the floor lift and sink under him like the deck of a great ship, and then there would be a heavy sloshing of sea water in the partitioned end of the room. His communicator was in there. A permanent post of Oganoon guards was also in there to make sure he didn't get near the communicator unless the Everliving decided to permit it. And the water covering most of the floor was there because the guards had to keep their leathery hides wet.

From the energy-screened ventilator window near the ceiling came dim sounds like the muted roaring of a beast. That and the periodic heaving of the floor were the only indications Ticos had been given for the past several days that the typhoons still blew outside. . . .

Rain squalls veiled half the sea below the aircar. It was storm season in the southern latitudes of Nandy-Cline . . . the horizon loomed blue-black ahead; heavy swirling cloud banks drove across the ocean to the south. The trim little car bucked suddenly in twisting torrents of air, was hauled

THE DEMON BREED

about on its controls and, for the moment, rode steady again along a southeasterly course.

Inside the cabin, Nile Etland stabbed at a set of buttons on the panel communicator, said sharply into the transmitter, "Giard Pharmaceuticals Station—come in! Nile Etland calling . . . Giard, come in!"

She waited a moment, tanned face intent. A hum began in the communicator, rose to a wavering howl, interspersed with explosive cracklings. Impatiently, Nile spun the filter control right, then left. Racketing noise erupted along the scale. She muttered bitter comment. Her fingers flicked over the call buttons, picked out another symbol.

"Danrich Patrol—Nile calling! Come in! Dan, can you *hear* me? *Come in!*"

Silence for an instant. Then meaningless sound spat and spluttered again. Nile's lips twisted in angry frustration. She muted the speaker, glanced down at the animal curled in a thick loop of richly gleaming brown fur on the floorboards beside her. It lifted a whiskered head, dark eyes watching Nile.

"Dan?" it asked, in a high thin voice.

"No Dan! No anybody!" snapped Nile. "We keep hitting a soup of static anywhere beyond twenty miles all around."

"Soup?"

"Forget it, Sweeting. We'll try calling the sledmen. Maybe they can help us find Ticos."

"Find Tikkos!" Sweeting agreed. The furred shape shifted, flowed, came upright. Bracing short sturdy forelegs against the control panel, Sweeting peered at the sections of seascape and sky in the viewscreens, looked over at Nile. Seven and a half feet in length from nose to the tip

20

of her muscular tail, she was the smaller of Nile's pair of mutant hunting otters. "Where's sledmen?"

"Somewhere ahead." Nile had swung the car fifteen degrees to the east. "Settle down."

The sled she'd sighted in the screens several minutes earlier presently came to view again, now only a few miles away. The car's magnification scanners showed a five hundred foot floatwood raft with flattened, streamlined superstructure, riding its runners twelve yards above the surging seas. The central heavy-weather keel was down, knifing through the waves between runners. On a day of less violence, the sled would have been drifting with an illusion of airy lightness over the water, keel withdrawn, sails spread. Now the masts were hauled flat to the deck, and it was the set of cannon drives along the sled's edges which sent it rushing toward the moving front of the storm. The rain-darkened afterdeck was emblazoned with a pair of deep-blue triangles—the Blue Guul symbol of the Sotira Fleet.

As the sled vanished below the next cloud bank, Nile switched the communicator to ten mile close-contact band, said into the transmitter, "Dr. Nile Etland of Giard Pharmaceuticals calling Sotira sled! Acknowledge, please!" Close-contact seemed to have stayed operational. And they should know her by name down there. The Sotira sleds did regular sea-harvest work for Giard.

The communicator said suddenly, "Captain Doncar of Sotira sled acknowledging. Go ahead, Dr. Etland. . . ."

"I'm in the air behind you," Nile announced. "May I come aboard?"

A moment of silence. Then Doncar's voice said, "If you

wish. But we'll be running through heavy storm in less than fifteen minutes."

"I know—I don't want to lose you in it."

"Come down immediately then," Doncar advised her. "We'll be ready for you."

They were. Almost before Nile could climb out of the aircar, half a dozen men in swimming gear, muscular naked backs glistening in the slashing rain, had the small vehicle strapped securely against the sled's deck beside a plastic-shrouded object which might be an oversized harpoon gun. It was a disciplined, practiced operation. As they stepped back, a brown-skinned girl, dressed down for the weather like the crewmen, hurried up from the central row of cabins. She shouted something almost lost in the din of wind and rain.

Nile turned. "Jath!"

"This way, Nile! Before the slop drowns us—"

They sprinted back to the cabins through the solid downpour. The otter loped easily after them, given plenty of room by the deck hands. Many of Sweeting's relatives preferred the unhampered freedom of Nandy-Cline's ocean to a domesticated life; and the seagoing mutant otters were known to any sledman at least by reputation. Nothing was gained by asking for trouble with them.

"In here!" Jath hauled open a door, slipped into the cabin behind Nile and the otter and let the door slam shut. Towels lay ready on a table; she tossed two to Nile, dabbed a third perfunctorily over her copper skin. Sweeting shook spray from her fur with a twist that spattered half the cabin. Nile mopped at her dripping coveralls, handed back one of the towels, used the other to dry hair, face and hands. "Thanks!"

"Doncar can't get away at the moment," Jath told her. "He asked me to find out what we can do for you. So—what brings you out in this weather?"

"I'm looking for somebody."

"Here?" There was startled surprise in Jath's voice.

"Dr. Ticos Cay."

A pause. "Dr. Cay is in *this* area?"

"He might be—" Nile checked momentarily. Jath, in a motion as quick as it was purposeful, had cupped her right hand to her ear, lowered it again.

They knew each other well enough to make the point of the gesture clear. Someone elsewhere on the sled was listening to what was being said in the cabin.

Nile gave Jath the briefest of understanding nods. Evidently there was something going on in this section of the sea which the Sotira sleds regarded as strictly sledman business. She was a mainlander, though a privileged one. An outsider.

She said, "I had a report from meteorological observers this morning about a major floatwood drift they'd spotted moving before the typhoons around here. The island Dr. Cay's been camping on could be part of that drift. . . ."

"You're not sure?"

"I'm not at all sure. I haven't been in touch with him for two months. But the Meral may have carried him this far south. I've been unable to get in contact with him. He's probably all right, but I've begun to feel worried."

Jath bit her lip, blue-green eyes staring at Nile's forehead. Then she shrugged. "You should be worried! But if he's on the floatwood the weather men saw, we wouldn't know it."

"Why not? . . . And why should I be worried?"

"Floatwood's gromgorru this season. So is the water twenty miles around any island. That's Fleet word."

Nile hesitated, startled. "When was the word given?"

"Five weeks ago."

Gromgorru . . . Sledman term for bad luck, evil magic. The malignant unknown. Something to be avoided. And something not discussed, under ordinary circumstances, with mainlanders. Jath's use of the term was deliberate. It was not likely to please the unseen listeners.

A buzzer sounded. Jath gave Nile a quick wink.

"That's for me." She started for the door, turned again. "We have Venn aboard. They'll want to see you now."

Alone with Sweeting, Nile scowled uneasily at the closed door. What the gromgorru business in connection with the floatwood islands was she couldn't imagine. But if Ticos Cay was in this ocean area—and her calculations indicated he shouldn't be too far away—she'd better be getting him out. . . .

2

Ticos cay had showed up unannounced one day at the Giard Pharmaceuticals Station on Nandy-Cline, to see Nile. He'd been her biochemistry instructor during her final university year on Orado. He was white-haired, stringy, bouncy, tough-minded, something of a genius, something of a crank, and the best all-around teacher she'd ever encountered. She was delighted to meet him again. Ticos informed her she was responsible for his presence here.

"In what way?" Nile asked.

"The research you've done on the floatwood."

Nile gave him a questioning look. She'd written over a dozen papers on Nandy-Cline's pelagic floatwood forests, forever on the move about the watery planet where one narrow continent and the polar ice massifs represented the only significant barriers to the circling tides of ocean. It was a subject on which she'd been acquiring first-hand information since childhood. The forests she'd studied most specially rode the great Meral Current down through the equatorial belt and wheeled with it far to the south. Many returned eventually over the same path, taking four to ten years to complete the cycle, until at length they were drawn off into other currents. Unless the polar ice closed about it permanently or it became grounded in mainland shallows, the floatwood organism seemed to know no natural death. It was an old species, old enough to have become the home of innumerable other species adjusted in a variety of ways to the climatic changes encountered in its migrations, and of temporary guests who attached themselves to forests crossing the ocean zones they frequented, deserting them again or dying as the floatwood moved beyond their ranges of temperature tolerance.

"It's an interesting subject," she said. "But—"

"You're wondering why I'd make a three weeks' trip out here to discuss the subject with you?"

"Yes, I am."

"It isn't all I had in mind," said Ticos. "I paid a visit to Giard's Central in Orado City a month or so ago. I learned, among other things, that there's a shortage of trained field biologists on Nandy-Cline."

"That's an understatement," said Nile.

"Evidently," Ticos remarked, "it hasn't hampered you too much. Your lab's held in high esteem by the home office."

"I know. We earn their high esteem by keeping way ahead of the competition. But for every new item we turn up with an immediate practical application for Giard, there are a thousand out there that remain unsuspected. The people who work for us are good collectors but they can't do instrument analysis and wouldn't know what to look for if they could. They bring in what you tell them to bring in. I still go out myself when I can, but that's not too often now."

"What's the problem with getting new hire?"

Nile shrugged. "The obvious one. If a man's a good enough biologist, he has his pick of jobs in the Hub. He'd probably make more here, but he isn't interested in coming all the way out to Nandy-Cline to do rough field work. I

. . . Ticos, *you* don't happen to be looking for a job here with Giard?"

He nodded. "I am, as a matter of fact. I believe I'm qualified, and I have my own analytical laboratory at the spaceport. Do you think your station manager would consider me?"

Nile blinked. "Parrol will snap you up, of course! . . . But I don't get it. How do you intend to fit this in with your university work?"

I resigned from the university early this year. About the job here—I do have a few conditions."

"What are they?"

"For one thing, I'll limit my work to the floatwood islands."

Why not, Nile thought. Provided they took adequate precautions. He looked in good physical shape, and she knew he'd been on a number of outworld field trips.

She nodded, said, "We can fit you up with a first-class staff of assistants. Short on scientific training but long on floatwood experience. Say ten or—"

"Uh-uh!" Ticos shook his head decidedly. "You and I will select an island and I'll set myself up there alone. That's Condition Two. It's an essential part of the project."

Nile stared at him. The multiformed life supported by the floatwood wasn't abnormally ferocious; but it existed because it could take care of itself under constantly changing conditions, which included frequent shifts in the nature of enemies and prey, and in the defensive and offensive apparatus developed to deal with them. For the uninformed human intruder such apparatus could turn into a wide variety of death traps. Their menace was for the most part as mindlessly impersonal as quicksand. But that didn't make them any less deadly.

"Ticos Cay," she stated, "you're out of your mind! You wouldn't last! Do you have any idea—"

"I do. I've studied your papers carefully, along with the rather skimpy material that's available otherwise on the planet's indigenous life. I'm aware there may be serious environmental problems. We'll discuss them. But solitude is a requirement."

"Why in the world should—"

"From a personal point of view, I'll be involved here primarily in longevity research."

She hesitated, said, "Frankly I don't see the connection."

Ticos grunted. "Of course you don't. I'd better start at the beginning."

"Perhaps you should. Longevity research . . ." Nile paused. "Is there some, uh, personal—"

"Is the life I'm interested in extending my own? Definitely. I'm at a point where it requires careful first-hand attention."

Nile felt startled. Ticos was lean but firmly muscled, agile and unwrinkled. In spite of his white hair, she hadn't considered him old. He might have been somewhat over sixty and not interested in cosmetic hormones. "You've begun extension treatments?" she asked.

"Quite a while ago," Ticos said dryly. "How much do you know about the assorted longevity techniques?"

"I have a general understanding of them, of course. But I've never made a special study of the subject. Nobody I've known has—" Her voice trailed off again.

"Don't let it embarrass you to be talking to a creaky ancient about it," Ticos said.

She stared at him. "How old *are* you?"

"Rather close to two hundred standard years. One of the Hub's most senior citizens, I believe. Not considering, of course, the calendar age of old-timers who resorted to long-sleep and are still around."

Two hundred years was the practical limit to the human biological life span. For a moment Nile didn't know what to say. She tried to keep shock from showing in her face. But perhaps Ticos noticed it because he went on quickly, his tone light. "It's curious, you know, that we still aren't able to do much better along those lines! Of course, during the war centuries there evidently wasn't much attention given to such impractical lines of research."

"Impractical?" Nile repeated.

"From the viewpoint of the species. The indefinite extension of individual life units isn't really too desirable in that respect. Natural replacements have obvious advantages. I can agree in theory. Nevertheless, I find myself resenting the fact that the theory should also apply to me. . . ."

He'd started resenting it some two decades ago. Up to then he'd been getting by exceptionally well on biochemical adjustments and gene manipulations, aided by occasional tissue transplants. Then trouble began—so gradually that it was a considerable while before he realized there was a real problem. He was informed at last that adjustment results were becoming increasingly erratic and that there was no known way of balancing them more accurately. Major transplants and the extensive use of synthetics would presently be required. It was suggested that he get his memory stores computerized and transferred to an information bank for reference purposes—and then perhaps check in for long-sleep.

Ticos found he didn't like any of the prospects. His interest level hadn't diminished noticeably, and he didn't care to have his activities curtailed by a progressively patched-up body or suspended indefinitely by longsleep. If he didn't take longsleep, he might make it past the two hundred year mark but evidently not by much. Previously he hadn't given a great deal of attention to regeneration research. Those problems were for other men—he had a large variety of pet projects of his own going. Now he thought he'd better start investigating the field and look for more acceptable alternatives to the prognosis offered him.

"You've been doing that for the past twenty years?" Nile asked.

"Very nearly. Some thousands of lines of research are involved. It makes for a lengthy investigation."

"I thought most of those lines of research were over on the crackpot side," she remarked.

"A great many are. I still had to check them out. One problem here is that nobody can prove his method is going to work out indefinitely—no method has been practiced long enough for that. For the same reason it's difficult to disprove the value of any approach, at least to those who believe in it. So egos and individualism run rampant in that area. Even the orthodox work isn't well coordinated."

"So I understand," Nile said. "You'd think the Federation would take a hand in it."

"You might think so," Ticos agreed. "However, there may be a consensus of opinion at Overgovernment levels that, because of economic and other factors, the unlimited prolongation of life in human beings would have questionable value. At any rate, while the Federation doesn't discourage longevity research, it doesn't actively support it. You could say it tolerates it."

"What about their own lives? They're human."

He shrugged. "They may be putting their trust in long-sleep—some happy future in which all such problems will be solved. I wouldn't know. Of course, a good many people suspect that if you're one of the elect, you'll have treatments that work indefinitely. It seems a little improbable. Anyway I'm betting largely on biochemistry now. The individual cells. Keep them cleared of degenerative garbage, and other problems may no longer be too significant. I made some improvements in that area a few years ago. An immediate result was improvements in myself. As a matter of fact, I've been given to understand they're probably the reason I'm still operational."

"You've written that up?" Nile asked.

"Not under my name. The university handles that end of it. I've kept the biochemical research going, but I've also been working on new slants since. It struck me frequently in the course of all this that our instincts evidently aren't in favor of letting us go on indefinitely."

She frowned. "What gives you that impression?"

"For one thing, the fact that we generally won't put out very much effort for it. A remarkable number of my earlier associates dropped out on treatments simply because they kept forgetting to do, or refused to do, the relatively simple things needed to stay alive. It was as though they'd decided it wasn't important enough and they couldn't be bothered."

Nile said doubtfully, "You aren't exaggerating?"

"No. It's a common picture. The instincts accept the life

and death cycle even when we're consciously opposed to it. They work for the species. The individual has significance to the species only to the point of maturity. The instincts support him until he's had an opportunity to pass along his genetic contribution. Then they start pulling him down. If a method eventually is developed to retain life and biological youth with *no* effort, it might be a different matter. Longsleep provides an illusion of that at present. But longsleep shelves the problem. I began to suspect longevity research itself is hampered by the instincts. And I'm not sure it isn't . . . we really *should* be farther along with it. At any rate, I decided to check with people who are interested in the less accessible areas of the mind. They're working in a major playground of the instincts, and they might have information. . . ."

He'd found two groups who were obtaining longevity and rejuvenation effects as a by-product of mental experimentation. One was the Psychovariant Association. Nile knew as much about their work as they'd chosen to publish in the digests she followed. They used assorted forcing procedures to extend and modify mental experience. "Don't they make heavy use of synthetics?" she asked.

Ticos nodded. "Yes. Not only to replace failing organs but to improve on healthy ones. That's their view of it. I don't fancy the approach myself. But they have systems of basic mind exercises directed at emotional manipulation. Longevity's a secondary interest, but they've accumulated plenty of evidence that the exercises support it. . . ."

The other project was a branch of the Federation's Psychology Service. Its goal was a total investigation of the mind and the gaining of conscious controls over its unconscious potential. The processes were elaborate. In the course of them, deep-reaching therapeutic adjustments were required and obtained. Physical regeneration frequently was a result—again not as a primary objective but as a beneficial side-effect.

Ticos decided this approach also went beyond his own aims. His interests were outward-directed; his mind was an efficient instrument for that purpose, and he demanded no more of it. However, the goals of both organizations were as definitely bent on overcoming normal human limitations as longevity research. They were aware of the type of inherent resistances he had suspected and had developed methods of dealing with them.

"The matter of mind-body interaction," he said. "I can learn to distinguish and control instinctual effects both in my mind and in associated physical processes. And that's what I've started to do."

He'd presented his problem to members of the two groups, and a modified individual schedule of mind-control exercises was worked out for him. He'd practiced them under direction until his mentors decided he was capable of continuing on his own. Then he'd closed out the final phases of his university work. His search for more effective biochemical serums would continue; he was convinced now it was the basic key to success.

"Keep the instincts from interfering and who knows—we might have it made!"

"Immortality?" asked Nile.

He gave her his quick grin. "Let's try for a thousand standard years first."

She smiled. "You almost have me believing you, Ticos!

33

And how does becoming a floatwood hermit fit in with it all?"

"Nandy-Cline evidently is a simmering hotbed of life. I know the general type of substances I'll be looking for next, and I think I'm at least as likely to find them here as anywhere else."

Nile nodded. "You might find almost anything here. Why make it a one-man job?"

"Planned solitude," said Ticos.

"What will that do for you?"

"The mind exercises. Does it seem to mean anything if I say that at the stages at which I'll now be working I step outside the standard mental patterns of the species?"

She considered. "It doesn't seem to mean much. Very advanced stuff, eh?"

"Depends on the viewpoint. The people I dealt with consider it basic. However, it's difficult work. There's seepage from other mind patterns about you, and if they're established human ones they jar you out of what you're doing. They're too familiar. It's totally disruptive. So until I become sufficiently stable in those practices, it's necessary to reduce my contacts with humanity to the absolute minimum."

Nile shrugged. "Well, that's obviously out of my line. Still, I'd think . . . you can't just go into a room somewhere and shut the doors?"

"No. Physical distance is required. Plenty of it."

"How long is it going to be required?"

"The estimates I've had range from three to four years."

"In the floatwood?"

"Yes. It's to be both my work place and my source of materials. I can't park myself in space somewhere and continue to do meaningful research. And I think that adequate preparations should reduce any risks I'll encounter to an acceptable level. A reasonable degree of risk, as a matter of fact, will be all to the good."

"In what way?"

"The threat of danger is a great awakener. The idea in this is to be thoroughly alert and alive—*not* shut away in a real or symbolical shell of some kind."

Nile reflected. "That makes a sort of sense," she agreed. She hesitated. "What's your present physical condition? I'll admit you look healthy enough. . . ."

"I'm healthier now than I was ten years ago."

"You don't need medical supervision?"

"I haven't needed it for several years. I've had one arterial replacement—the cultured product. That was quite a while ago. Otherwise, except for a few patches from around the same and earlier periods, my internal arrangements are my own. Nothing to worry about in that department."

Nile sighed.

"Well—we'll still have to convince Parrol it isn't suicide. But you're hired, Ticos. Make it a very high salary and nail down your terms, including your interests in anything that could classify as a longevity serum. After we've settled that, I'll start briefing you on the kind of difficulties you're likely to run into on your island. That can't be done in a matter of days. It's going to take weeks of cramming and on-the-spot demonstrations."

Ticos winked at her. "That's why I'm here."

She made it a very stiff cramming course. And Ticos turned out to be as good a student as he'd been an instructor. He had an alert, curious mind, an extraordinarily retentive memory. Physically he proved to be tough and

resilient. Nile kept uprating his survival outlook, though she
didn't mention it. Some things, of course, she couldn't
teach him. His gunmanship was only fair. He learned to
use a climb-belt well enough to get around safely; but to
develop anything resembling real proficiency with the device required long practice. She didn't even attempt to in-
struct him in water skills. The less swimming he did around
floatwood the better.

They moved about the Meral from one floatwood drift
to another, finally selected a major island complex which
seemed to meet all requirements. A shelter, combining
Ticos' living quarters, laboratory and storerooms, was con-
structed and his equipment moved in. A breeding group
of eight-inch protohoms and cultures of gigacells would
provide him with his principal test material; almost every
known human reaction could be duplicated in them, usually
with a vast advantage in elapsed time. The structure was
completely camouflaged. Sledmen harvesting parties probably would be about the island from time to time, and Ticos
didn't want too many contacts with them. If he stayed inside until such visitors left again, he wouldn't be noticed.

He had a communicator with a coded call symbol. Unless he got in touch with her, Nile was to drop by at eight
week intervals to pick up what he had accumulated for the
Giard lab and leave supplies. He wished to see no one else.
Parrol shook his head at the arrangement; but Nile made no
objections. She realized that by degrees she'd become
fiercely partisan in the matter. If Ticos Cay wanted to take
a swing at living forever, on his feet and looking around,
instead of fading out or sliding off into longsleep, she'd
back him up, however he went about it. Up to this point he
hadn't done badly.

And somewhat against general expectations then, he lasted. He made no serious mistakes in his adopted environment, seemed thoroughly satisfied with his life as a hermit, wholly immersed in his work. The home office purred over his bi-monthly reports. Assorted items went directly to the university colleagues who had taken over his longevity project there. They also purred. When Nile had seen him last, he'd been floating along the Meral for eighteen months, looked hale and hearty and ready to go on for at least the same length of time. His mind exercises, he informed Nile, were progressing well. . . .

3

THERE WERE three men waiting in the central cabin of the Sotira sled to which Jath presently conducted Nile. She knew two of them from previous meetings, Fiam and Pelad. Both were Venn, members of the Fleet Venntar, the sledman center of authority: old men and former sled captains. Their wrinkled sun-blackened faces were placid; but they were in charge. On a sled a Venn's word overrode that of the captain.

Doncar, the sled captain, was the third. Quite young for his rank, intense, with a look of controlled anger about him. Bone-tired at the moment. But controlling that too.

Jath drew the door shut behind Nile and the otter, took a seat near Doncar. She held a degree of authority not far below that of the others here, having spent four years at a Hub university, acquiring technical skills of value to her people. Few other sledmen ever had left Nandy-Cline. Their forebears had been independent space rovers who settled on the water world several generations before the first Federation colonists. By agreement with the Federation, they retained their independence and primary sea rights. But there had been open conflict between the fleets and mainland groups in the past, and the sleds remained traditionally suspicious of the mainland and its ways.

Impatience tingled in Nile, but she knew better than to hurry this group. She answered Pelad's questions, repeating essentially what she had told Jath.

"You aren't aware of Dr. Cay's exact location?" Pelad inquired. Ticos had become a minor legend among the sled people who knew of his project.

Nile shook her head.

"I can't say definitely that he's within four hundred miles of us," she said. "This is simply the most likely area to start looking for him. When I'm due to pay him a visit, I give him a call and he tells me what his current position is. But this time he hasn't responded to his call symbol."

She added, "Of course there've been intensive communication interferences all the way in to the mainland in recent weeks. But Dr. Cay still should have picked up my signal from time to time. I've been trying to get through to him for the past several days."

Silence for a moment, then Pelad said, "Dr. Etland, does the mainland know what is causing the interferences?"

The question surprised, then puzzled her. The interferences were no novelty; their cause was known. The star type which tended to produce water worlds also produced such disturbances. On and about Nandy-Cline the communication systems otherwise in standard use throughout the Federation were rarely operable. Several completely new systems had been developed and combined to deal with the problem. Among them, only the limited close-contact band was almost entirely reliable.

Pelad and the others here were as aware of that as she. Nile said, "As far as I know, no special investigation has been made. Do the sleds see some unusual significance in the disturbances?"

"There are two views," Jath told her quietly. "One of them is that some of the current communication blocks are gromgorru. Created deliberately by an unknown force. Possibly by an unnatural one. . . ."

Pelad glanced at Jath, said to Nile, "The Venntar has decreed silence in this. But young mouths open easily. Perhaps too easily. We may have reason to believe there is something in the sea that hates men. There are those who hear voices in the turmoil that smothers our instruments. They say they hear a song of hate and fear." He shrugged. "I won't say what I think—as yet I don't know what to think." He looked at Fiam. "Silence might have been best, but it has been broken. Dr. Etland is a proven friend of the sleds."

Fiam nodded. "Let the captain tell it to our guest."

Doncar grinned briefly. "Tell it as I see it?"

"As you see it, Doncar. We know your views. We shall listen."

"Very well." Doncar turned to Nile. "Dr. Etland, so far you've been asked questions and given no explanation. Let me ask one more question. Could human beings cause such communication problems?"

"By duplicating the solar effect locally?" Nile hesitated, nodded. "It should be possible. Is there reason to believe it's being done?"

"Some of us think so," Doncar said dryly. "We've lost men."

"Lost them?"

"They disappear. . . . Work parties harvesting a floatwood island—small surface craft and submersibles in the immediate vicinity of floatwood. Later no traces are found. Whenever this occurred, communication in the area was completely disrupted."

"To keep the men from reporting attackers?"

"That's what's suspected," Doncar said. "It's happened

too regularly to make coincidences seem probable. You understand, Dr. Etland, that this isn't a problem which affects only the Sotira sleds. There have been similar disappearances near floatwood islands in many sea areas of late."

Nile asked for details, her mind beginning to race. She and Parrol were known as accomplished trouble shooters. They considered it part of their job; it was in Giard's interest to keep operations moving as smoothly as possible on Nandy-Cline. The sledmen had benefited by that in the past, as had the mainland. And trouble—man-made trouble—was always likely to arise. The planet's natural riches were tempting . . . particularly when some new discovery was made and kept concealed.

This then might be such trouble on a large scale. The pattern of disappearances had begun north of the equator, spread down through the Sotira range. It had started three months ago. And the purpose, she thought, presumably was to accomplish precisely what it had accomplished—to keep the sleds away from the islands. For a period long enough to let whoever was behind the maneuver clear out whatever treasure of rare elements or drugs they'd come across and be gone again.

No local organization was big enough to pull off such a stunt. But a local organization backed by a Hub syndicate could be doing it—

Gromgorru? Nile shrugged mentally. The deeps of Nandy-Cline were only sketchily explored; great sections of the ocean floor remained unmapped. But she had very little faith in unknown malignant powers. In all her experience, whenever there was real mischief afoot, human operators had been found behind it.

The others here were less sure. There was something like

superstitious dread unspoken but heavy in the air of this cabin, with the deck shuddering underfoot and the typhoon howling and thudding beyond the thick walls. She thought Doncar and Jath weren't free of it. Jath had acquired a degree of sophistication very uncommon among the sledmen. But she still was a woman of the sea sleds, whose folk had drunk strangeness from the mysteries of ocean and space for centuries. Space life and sea life didn't breed timid people. But it bred people who would not go out of their way to pit themselves against forces they could not understand.

Nile said to Pelad, "You spoke of those who hear voices of hate when the communicators are blanked out."

The Venn's eyes flickered for an instant. He nodded.

"Do the other-seeing"—Nile used the sledmen term for psi sensitives—"connect these voices with the disappearances in the floatwood drifts?"

Pelad hesitated, said, "No. Not definitely."

"They haven't said this is a matter men can't handle?"

"They haven't said it," Pelad agreed slowly. "They don't know. They only know what they've told us."

So the witch doctors had suggested just enough to stall action. Nile said, "Then there may very well be two things here. One, what the other-seeing sense. The second, a human agency which is responsible for the present trouble in the floatwood. What if the sleds learn that is the case?"

Doncar said, "There're six spaceguns mounted on this sled, Dr. Etland, and men trained in their use."

"I myself," said Pelad, "am one of those men."

Fiam added, "There are two other Sotira sleds not far from here. Each armed with four spaceguns—very old guns but in excellent working order." He gave Nile a brief smile. "The mainland may recall them."

"The mainland does," Nile agreed. "You'll fight if you know you're not fighting gromgorru?"

"We'll fight men," Pelad said. "We have always fought men when necessary. But it would be unwise to challenge blindly an evil which may not be affected by guns and which might be able to wipe the sleds from the sea." His face darkened again. "Some believe there is such an evil at no great distance from us."

She must be careful at this point. Still, so far, so good. In their minds the Venn were committed now to fight, if shown an enemy with whom weapons could deal. Too early to ask them to cooperate with mainland authorities in this. Their distrust was too deep.

Five minutes later she knew what she must do. Her immediate concern was to get Ticos out of harm's way. The big floatwood drift for which she had been looking was eighty miles south of this point. A Sotira seiner had been missing for several days, and the last reports from it indicated it might have moved too near the drift in the storm and become another victim of whatever menace haunted floatwood waters. Doncar's sled had been hunting for the seiner in the vicinity of the drift but found no clue to what had happened. The search had now been abandoned.

There were no other sizable floatwood islands within two hundred miles. Therefore the one on which Ticos had set up his project should be part of the drift. It was almost a certainty. If she took her aircar there at once, she could identify the island while daylight remained. The risk shouldn't be too great. Aircars hadn't come under attack, and the one she had was a fast sports model. If there was a suggestion of hostile action, she could clear out very quickly. If there wasn't, she'd try to wake Ticos up on the close-

43

contact channel and establish what the situation down there was. She might have him out inside an hour.

If that didn't work, she wasn't equipped to do much more by herself; and she needed reinforcements in any case before trying to determine who might have been turning the floatwood islands into death traps.

She asked, "Can you get a message through to the mainland for me?"

They nodded, the Venn warily. Jath said, "It may take a number of hours. But so far the fleets have always been able to relay messages through disturbance areas."

Fiam inquired, "What's the message, Dr. Etland? And to whom will it go?"

"It goes to Danrich Parrol," Nile told him. "The Giard Station will be able to locate him." She couldn't become too specific about gromgorru matters or the message would be blocked before it reached the mainland. "Give Parrol the location of the floatwood drift south of us. I'll wait for him there. Tell him I may have a problem getting Dr. Cay off his island, and that I'd like him to come out with full trouble-shooting equipment—"

"*And* Spiff!" a thin voice interrupted emphatically from the corner of the room.

The sledmen looked around, startled. Sweeting blinked at them, began nosing her chest fur disinterestedly. People who didn't know Sweeting well frequently were surprised by the extent to which she followed the details of human discussions.

"And Spiff, of course," Nile agreed. "If we find out what's been happening around the floatwood, we'll try to get word to you at once."

Fiam nodded quickly. "Six hours from now we'll have a

44

racing sled in the drift. Any close-contact messages should be picked up. Code Sotira-Doncar, on the sledmen frequencies. . . ."

"The Great Palach Koll," said the demon on the platform, "has persuaded the Everliving to permit him to test the Tuvela Theory."

Ticos Cay didn't reply immediately. His visitor was the Palach Moga, one of the Everliving, though of lower grade than the Great Palachs and somewhere between them and the Oganoon in physical structure, about Ticos' size and weight. Moga didn't squat but stood upright, long hopping legs stretched out, and walked upright when he walked, with short careful awkward steps. His torso was enclosed in an intricate close-worked harness of silver straps. In what was happening here he and Ticos Cay had become cautious allies. Ticos was aware that the alliance might be of very temporary nature.

"I was under the impression," he told Moga, "that the Voice of Caution was able to keep the reckless demands of the Great Palach from being given a hearing."

Moga's speaking slit twisted in agitation.

"We have done it until now," he said. "But the Great Palach has assumed control of the Voice of Action. He accused his predecessor of a Violation of Rules, and the Everliving found the accusation valid. The predecessor was granted the death of a Palach. You must understand that in his new position Koll's demands can no longer be silenced."

"Yes, I see . . ." Advancement usually came the hard way among the demons. Two favored methods were a ritualized form of assassination and having one's superior convicted of a Violation of Rules. They had the same practical result.

Ticos swallowed. Bad—very bad. . . . He leaned back against the worktable to avoid revealing that his legs were trembling. "How does the Great Palach propose to test the Tuvela Theory?"

"The Guardian Etland is again attempting to contact you," Moga said.

"Yes, I know." The communicator in the partitioned end of the room had signaled half a dozen times during the past half hour.

"The signals," Moga explained, "are on the cambi channel."

The close-contact band! Ticos said thickly, "She already is in the area?"

"Could anyone else be seeking for you here?"

"No."

"Then it is the Guardian. There is a human airvehicle high overhead. It is very small but rides the storm well. It moves away, returns again."

"The island growth has changed since she was here last," said Ticos. "She may not have determined yet on which of these islands I should be!" He added urgently, "This gives us a chance to forestall actions by Koll! I have the Guardian's call symbol—"

Moga gave the whistle of absolute negation.

"It is now quite impossible to approach your communicator," he said. "I would die if I attempted it unless it were under open orders of the Everliving. Koll will be allowed to carry out his plan. He has arranged tests to determine whether a Tuvela is a being such as the Tuvela Theory conjectures it to be. The first test will come while the Guardian is still in the air. At a selected moment the Great Palach will have a device activated which is directed at her vehicle. If she responds promptly and correctly, the vehicle will be incapacitated, but the Guardian will not be harmed. If she does not respond promptly and correctly, she dies at that point."

Moga stared at Ticos a moment. "The significance of her death, of course, will be the Everliving's conclusion that Tuvelas lack the basic qualities ascribed to them. The Great Plan is now in balance. If the balance is to shift again in favor of the Voice of Caution, the Guardian must not fail. Her class is being judged in her. If she fails, the Voice of Action attains full control.

"Let us assume she passes this first test. The vehicle will descend to a point where Koll's personal company of Oganoon await the Guardian. Unless she has weapons of great effectiveness, she must surrender to them. Note that if she does not surrender and is killed, it will be judged a failure. A Tuvela, as Tuvelas are assumed to be, will not make such mistakes. A Tuvela will surrender and await better opportunities to act to advantage."

Ticos nodded slowly. "I'll be able to speak to the Guardian if she is captured?"

"No, Dr. Cay. Only the Great Palach Koll will speak to the Guardian following her capture. The tests will continue at once and with increasing severity until the Guardian either dies or proves to the Everliving beyond all doubt that the Tuvela Theory is correct in all its implications—specifically, that the Tuvelas, individually and as a class, are the factor which must cause us, even at this last moment, to halt and reverse the Great Plan. Koll is staking his life on his belief that she will fail. If she fails, he will have proved his point. The Everliving will hesitate no longer. And the final stages of the Plan will be initiated."

"In brief," Ticos said slowly, "the Great Palach intends to discredit the Tuvela Theory by showing he can torture the Guardian to death and add her to his collection of trophies?"

"Yes. That is his announced plan. The torture, of course, is an approved form of test. It is in accord with tradition."

Ticos stared up at him, trying to conceal his complete dismay. There was no argument he could advance. This was the way they were conditioned to think. Before a Palach became a Palach he submitted to painful tests which few survived. As he progressed toward the ultimate form of existence which was a Great Palach, he was tested again and again. It was their manner of evaluation, of judgment. Ticos had convinced a majority of them that Tuvelas were at least their human counterpart. Some were convinced, however unwillingly, that the counterpart was superior to the greatest of the Great Palachs—opponents too deadly to be challenged. Koll's move was designed to nullify that whole structure of thought. . . .

"I'll keep you informed of what occurs, Dr. Cay," Moga concluded. "If you have suggestions which might be useful in this situation, have word sent to me immediately. Otherwise we now see no way to block Koll's purpose—unless the Guardian herself proves able to do it. Let us hope that she does."

The Palach turned, moved off down the walkway toward the exit door. Ticos gazed after him. There was a leaden feeling of helplessness throughout his body. For the moment it seemed difficult even to stir from where he stood.

He didn't doubt that Nile Etland was the operator of the aircar they were watching—and he had been hoping very much she wouldn't arrive just yet.

Given even another two weeks, he might have persuaded

the Everliving through the Voice of Caution to cancel the planned attack on Nandy-Cline and withdraw from the planet. But Nile's arrival had precipitated matters and Koll was making full use of the fact. The one way in which Ticos could have warned her off and given her a clue to what was happening was closed completely.

Four words would have done it, he thought. Four words, and Nile would have known enough, once he'd switched on the communicator. He'd made preparations to ensure nobody was going to stop him before he got the four words out.

But now—without Moga's help, without the permission of the Everliving—he simply couldn't get to the communicator. It wasn't a question of the guards. He'd made other preparations for the guards. It was the devastatingly simple fact that the partitioning wall was twelve feet high and that there was no door in it. Ticos knew too well that he was no longer in any condition to get over the wall and to the communicator in time to do any good. They'd turn him off before he turned it on. He didn't have the physical strength and coordination left to be quick enough for such moves. . . .

If Nile had arrived a couple of weeks earlier, he could have done it. He'd counted then on being able to do it. But there'd been a few too many of their damned pain treatments since.

And if she'd delayed coming out by just two weeks, no warning might have been necessary.

But she was punctual as usual—right on time!

Well, Ticos told himself heavily, at least he'd arranged matters so that they wouldn't simply blast her out of the air as she came down to the island. It left her a slim chance.

However, it seemed time to start thinking in terms of last-ditch operations—for both of them. He had his preparations made there too. But they weren't very satisfactory ones. . . .

"Hungry," Sweeting announced from the aircar's floor beside Nile.

"So starve," Nile said absently. Sweeting opened her jaws, laughed up at her silently.

"Go down, eh?" she suggested. "Catch skilt for Nile, eh? Nile hungry?"

"Nile isn't. Go back to sleep. I have to think."

The otter snorted, dropped her head back on her forepaws, pretended to close her eyes. Sweeting's kind might be the product of a geneticist's miscalculation. Some twenty years before, a consignment of hunting otter cubs had reached Nandy-Cline. They were a development of a preserved Terran otter strain, tailored for an oceanic existence. The coastal rancher who'd bought the consignment was startled some months later when the growing cubs began to address him in a slurrily chopped-up version of the Hub's translingue. The unexpected talent didn't detract from their value. The talkative cubs, playful, affectionate, handsomely pelted, sold readily, were distributed about the sea coast ranches and attained physical maturity in another year and a half. As water hunters or drivers and protectors of the sea herds, each was considered the equivalent of half a dozen trained men. Adults, however, sooner or later tended to lose interest in their domesticated status and exchanged it for a feral life in the sea, where they thrived and bred. During the past few years sledmen had reported encounters with sizable tribes of wild otters. They still spoke in translingue.

Nile's pair, hand-raised from cubhood, had stayed. She wasn't quite sure why. Possibly they were as intrigued by her activities as she was by theirs. On some subjects her intellectual processes and theirs meshed comfortably. On others there remained a wide mutual lack of comprehension. She suspected, though she'd never tried to prove it, that their overall intelligence level was very considerably higher than was estimated.

She was holding the aircar on a southwest course, surface scanners shifting at extreme magnification about the largest floatwood island in the drift, two miles below, not quite three miles ahead. It looked very much like the one Ticos Cay had selected. Minor differences could be attributed to adaptive changes in the growth as the floatwood moved south. There were five major forest sections arranged roughly like the tips of a pentacle. The area between them, perhaps a mile across, was the lagoon, a standard feature of the islands. Its appearance was that of a shallow lake choked with vegetation, a third of the surface covered by dark green leafy pads flattened on the water. The forests, carrying the semiparasitical growth which clustered on the floatwood's thick twisted boles, towered up to six hundred feet about the lagoon, living walls of almost indestructible toughness and density. The typhoon battering through which they had passed had done little visible damage. Beneath the surface they were linked by an interlocking net of ponderous roots which held the island sections clamped into a single massive structure.

The island was moving slowly to the south, foam-streaked swells running past it on either side. This might be the southern fringe of the typhoon belt. The sky immediately overhead was clear, a clean deep blue. But violent gusts still shook the car, and roiling cloud banks rode past on all sides.

Ticos Cay's hidden arboreal laboratory should be in the second largest section of the floatwood structure, about a third of the way in on the seaward side. He wasn't responding to close-contact communicator signals; but he might be there in spite of his silence. In any case it was the place to start looking. There'd been no sign of intruders—which didn't mean they weren't there. The multiple canopies of the forests could have concealed an army. But intruders could be avoided.

Nile thought she might be able to handle this without waiting for Parrol. It was late afternoon now, and even if there were no serious delays in getting her message to him, it would be at best the middle of the night before he could make it out here. To drop down openly to the floatwood would be asking for trouble, of course, though there had been no reports of attacks on aircars as yet. But she could circle south, go down to sea level, submerge the car and maneuver it back underwater to the island through the weed beds which rode the Meral. If she'd had her jet diving rig with her, she wouldn't have hesitated. She could have left the car a couple of miles out, gone in at speed and brought Ticos out with her if he was in his hideaway, with almost no risk of being noticed by whoever else might be about. But she didn't have the rig along. That meant working the car in almost to the island, a more finicky operation.

But it could be done. The submerged weed jungles provided the best possible cover against detection instruments.

Nile checked course and altitude, returned her attention to the magnification scanners. Everything down there looked normal. There was considerable animal activity about the lagoon, including clouds of the flying kesters which filled the role of sea and shore birds in Nandy-Cline's ecological pattern. In the ocean beyond the floatwood at the left, two darkly gleaming torpedo-shaped bodies appeared intermittently at the surface. They were kesters too, but wingless giants: sea-havals, engaged in filling their crops with swarms of skilts. Their presence was another good indication that this was Ticos' island. There'd been a sea-haval rookery concealed in the forest section next to the one he'd selected—

An engine control shrieked warning, and a sullen roaring erupted about them. Nile saw a red line in the fuel release gauge surge up toward explosion as her hand flicked out and cut the main engine switch.

The shrieking whistle and the roar of energies gone wild subsided together. Losing momentum, the car began to drop.

"Nile?"

"We're in trouble, Sweeting." The otter was on her feet, neck fur erect, eyes shifting about. But Sweeting knew enough to stay quiet in emergencies that were in Nile's department.

Energy block . . . it could be malfunction. But that type of malfunction occurred so rarely it had been years since she'd heard of a case.

Someone hidden in the floatwood had touched the car with a type of weapon unknown to her, was bringing her down. The car's built-in antigrav patterns would slow their descent. But—

Nile became very busy.

When she next looked at the altimeter, it told her she

had approximately three minutes left in the air. Wind pressure meanwhile had buffeted the car directly above the island, a third of the way out across the lagoon. That would have been the purpose of killing her engines at the exact moment it was done. When the car splashed into the lagoon's vegetation, she'd find a reception committee waiting.

She was in swim briefs by now for maximum freedom of action in water or in the floatwood. Fins and a handkerchief-sized breather mask lay on the seat. Most of the rest of what she was taking along had been part of the floatwood kit she'd flung into the back of the car on leaving the Giard Station. Various items were attached to a climb-belt about her waist—knife, lightweight UW gun, grip sandals, a pouch containing other floatwood gear she didn't have time to sort over. The otter caller she used to summon Sweeting and Spiff from a distance was fastened to her wrist above her watch. Her discarded clothing was in a waterproof bag.

"Remember what you're to do?"

"Yesss!" Sweeting acknowledged with a cheery hiss, whiskers twitching.

Sweeting would remember. They were going to meet some bad guys. Not at all a novel experience. Sweeting would keep out of sight and trouble until Nile had more specific instructions for her.

The bad guys hadn't showed yet. But they must be in the lagoon, headed for the area where the car seemed about to come down. It was rocking and lurching in the gusts toward a point some three hundred yards from the nearest floatwood. Not at all where Nile wanted it to go. But she might be able to improve her position considerably.

She sat quiet throughout the last moments, estimating the

force of the wind, eyes shifting between the altimeter and a landing area she'd selected on the far side of the water. Then, a hundred yards from the surface, she pushed down a stud which slid out broad glide-vanes to either side of the car.

The fringes of a typhoon were no place for unpowered gliding. Like the blow of a furious fist, wind slammed the vehicle instantly over on its side. Seconds of wild tumbling followed. But she had the momentum now to return some control of the car's motion to her. To hostile watchers in the lagoon and the floatwood it must have looked like a futile and nearly suicidal attempt to escape—as it was intended to look. She didn't want them to start shooting. Twice she seemed within inches of being slammed head-on into the water, picked up altitude at the last instant. Most of the width of the lagoon lay behind her at that point, and a section of forest loomed ahead again. A tall stand of sea reeds, perhaps three hundred yards across, half enclosed by gnarled walls of floatwood, whirled by below.

Wind force swept the car down once more, too fast, too far to the right. Nile shifted the vane controls. The car rose steeply, heeled over, swung sideways, its momentum checked—and that was almost exactly where she wanted to be. She slapped another stud. The vanes folded back into the vehicle. It began to drop, antigrav effect taking over. Nile reached for the fins, snapped them on her feet. Green tops of the reeds whipped suddenly about the car. She drew the transparent breather mask over her face, pressed its audio plugs into her ears. Car door open, set on lock . . . dense vegetation swaying jerkily with wet crashing sounds on all sides as the car descended through it—

Thump and splash!

55

Sweeting slithered past Nile's feet, flowed down over the doorsill, vanished into the lagoon without a sound. Nile pitched the clothing bag through the door, swung about on the seat, slid out into cool water. Turning, she caught a handgrip on the side of the car, reached up, slammed the door shut on its lock.

She saw the bag floating beside her, caught its strap and went down. . . .

4

THE SEA REEDS, rising from layers of muck packed into the matted root system of the island thirty feet below, grew thick and strong. Almost in moments after leaving the car, Nile knew she was relatively safe from immediate pursuit. On her way across the lagoon she'd had a flashing glimpse of an enclosed boat coming about in a tight circle among the pads to follow her. It wouldn't be long before it reached the reeds, and it might have divers aboard. In open water a jet diver advancing behind a friction-cutting field would have overhauled her in seconds. But jet rigs gave little real advantage when it came to slipping in and out of slime-slick dense growth; and if one had been in operation within a hundred yards, her audio plugs would have distinguished its thin hissing through the medley of sea sounds. She moved on quickly toward the forest. Small life scuttled and flicked away from her gliding shape. A school of eight-inch skilts exploded suddenly about her in a spray of silver glitters. . . . Sweeting, out of sight but somewhere nearby, might have turned aside for a fast snack. Something large and dark stirred ahead; a dorashen, some five hundred pounds of sluggish ugliness, black armor half concealed by a rusty fur of parasites, was backing off from her advance, pulling itself up along the reed stems, multiple jaws working in menacing snaps.

Sudden darkening of the water told her she'd reached the base of the forest. The reed growth ended and thick twisted floatwood trunks appeared through murky dimness. She stroked up to them, paused to look back. A dim regular rumbling had begun in the audio pickups. The sound of engines. But they weren't close.

Ticos Cay's hidden dwelling was less than a quarter-mile from here. Getting there unobserved would be the next move. A few minutes later, deep within the forest, in the maze of dark caverns formed by huge supporting trunks above the submerged roots, Nile lifted her head above the surging ocean surface, pulled off the breather. The otter's head appeared a dozen feet away.

"People here?" Nile asked.

"Smell no people."

"Boats?"

"Skilt boat. Coming slow."

"How big?"

"Big as three cars, heh."

No divers, and nobody upwind of them in the forest. Sweeting used nostrils in air, sensitive olfactories in the lining of her mouth in water. What she couldn't scent usually wasn't there. Skilt boat meant a submersible. It might have been the boat Nile had glimpsed in the lagoon. When Sweeting saw it, it was approaching the reed bed under water. Its crew should discover the ditched aircar in not too many minutes.

"Kill?" the otter asked.

"Not yet. Go back and watch what they're doing till I call you."

Sweeting vanished. Nile moved on through dark shifting water, avoiding contact with the giant trunks. They were coated with slime, heavily populated with crawling things. Not a pleasant place to be; but this level provided a quick route to the seaward side of the forest, and she intended to make her ascent from there. Presently she saw daylight flash intermittently through the snaky tangles of floatwood ahead.

Far enough. . . . She found a place to get out of the water, scrambled up to a horizontal perch and knotted the strap of the bag containing her discarded coveralls and other personal items around a spike of wood. The fewer clues to the car's occupants left for investigators, the better. She exchanged fins for grip sandals, fastened the fins to her climb-belt, switched the belt to its quarter-weight setting and stood up on the trunk.

There was a partial gravity shield about her now. Ordinary progress in a floatwood forest was an activity somewhere between mountaineering and tree climbing. With a climb-belt and sufficient practice in its use, it became not much more arduous than motion along level ground. Nile started up. The forest had no true floor, but a thick carpet of parasitic growth, trailing drinking roots to the sea, stretched out overhead. She pushed through the stuff, came into a relatively open area.

She stood glancing about, letting senses and mind adjust again to what was here. It was long-familiar territory. She'd been born in one of the shallows settlements of Nandy-Cline, halfway around the globe from the mainland; and whenever one of the swimming islands moved near, her people had gone to harvest from it what was in season, taking their children along to teach them the floatwood's bounty and perils. Making the islands the subject of extensive studies later on had been a natural consequence.

Though this was less densely growth-infested than the central forest levels, vision was restricted to at most a hundred feet in any direction. In the filtered half-light, the host organism was represented by unbranched reddish-brown boles, sloping and twisting upward—enormously massive, as they had to be to support all the rest. Sprouting or hanging from the trunks, or moving slowly along their coarse-furred surface, was the many-shaped secondary growth, in the inhis and tacapu categories, with plant or plant-animal characteristics. Gliding and hopping through the growth, fluttering about it, were small specimens of the animal population.

Nile's eyes and nostrils took it all in with only superficial conscious responses. A definite conscious reaction would come if she encountered something she didn't know or knew might harm her—or if she detected any trace of the intruders who had forced her down from the sky. Listening was a waste of effort; the booming winds drowned minor sounds. She started up the ascending curve of the trunk by which she had climbed from the sea. Presently it branched, then branched again. Now the floatwood's great oblong leaves began to appear among the other growth, shifting green curtains which closed vision down to the next few dozen steps ahead. It was more to her advantage than not. In the constant stirring, her lean body, tanned almost to the tint of the floatwood branches, would be next to impossible to detect if hostile watchers were about.

She was nearly four hundred feet above the ocean before sunlight began to play through the forest in wavering flashes, filtered through the canopy above. By then Nile was moving along an interlaced network of lesser branches. She knew she was somewhat above Ticos' dwelling and had been watching for its camouflaged outlines in the vegetation below. It was a sizable structure, but anyone who didn't know it was there might stare at it for minutes and not realize what he saw. It had been built of the materials growing about it and blended into them.

A great wet mass of fernlike stuff, sadly bent and tattered by the typhoons, caught at Nile's memory. The hideout should be thirty feet below, off to the left.

She reached the soggy greenery, clambered through, found a spot where she could look down. Nothing but more waving growth beneath her. She jumped over to a sloping trunk, caught at it with flexing grip sandals and hands, moved along to a horizontally jutting branch and stepped out on it to look around the trunk.

A broad spear of sunlight blazed past her, directly into the concealed entrance of the hideout. A naked man sat cross-legged in the entrance, staring up, mouth stretched wide as if in a frozen shriek of laughter.

Nile's next awareness—at the moment it seemed a simultaneous one—was of the UW in her hand, stubby muzzle pointed down at the grotesquely distended mouth of the figure.

The figure didn't move. For seconds then, neither did she. The eyes seemed fixed on her and her skin crawled with something very close to superstitious terror. The sunlight winked out suddenly. The forest shook and groaned in renewed surges of wind.

She was looking at a dead man, her mind told her belatedly. Not Ticos; he didn't show the slightest resemblance to Ticos . . . but what had frozen this unknown dead man here in that position, head twisted back, facial muscles distorted into an expression of grisly mirth? Her eyes began to shift about, returning every few seconds to the seated shape, as if she expected it to gain sudden life and come leaping up at her. The forest boomed, danced, rustled and snapped in the wind. She saw and heard nothing else. The figure remained unmoving. It had been there unmoving, she decided, for a considerable time. Days, at least. It was streaked with dirt, as if rain had run down on it and it had dried while the storm whipped forest debris about it, and rain presently washed it again.

She stepped back behind the trunk, moved down along it. A minute later her left hand carefully parted the cluster of plants encircling the platform to let her look beyond the man-shape into the structure. The entrance door was gone. Not torn away by storm violence. Removed deliberately. The entrance had been widened, cut back on either side.

The interior was dim, but part of the wall lighting was on, and after a moment she could see enough. Except for a few tables and wall shelves, the place seemed to have been stripped. The partitions were gone; only the thick outer framework remained. But the structure wasn't empty. There might be between twenty and thirty of them inside. They crouched on hands and knees, squatted, lay about. Their rigid immobility said there was no more life in them than in the figure on the platform. Nile moved slowly forward, gun out before her.

She paused by the seated man in the entrance, prodded his shoulder with a finger. The skin was cool, gummy; the flesh beneath it unyielding as lead. She started past, checked again, stomach contracting. A wide gash laid open the figure's back. It appeared to have been gutted completely through the gash. She stared a moment, went inside.

The others weren't very different. Ticos wasn't one of them. Dead eyes stared at Nile as she moved among the bodies. Dead mouths snarled, pleaded, grinned. All were savagely mutilated in one way or another. A few had been women. One of the women had the Blue Guul symbol of the Sotira sleds etched on her forehead—a good luck charm. Several wall sections were still covered with Ticos Cay's scribbled work notations and sketches. Nothing else of his seemed here. Nothing else seemed to be here at all except what the wet winds had swept in through the entrance. . . .

Then her eyes checked on something the wind hadn't blown in. It sat in the shadows on a wall shelf to one side of what had been the main room. Puzzled, she went slowly over to it.

It looked like a featureless black cloth figure, a hooded lumpy little doll, less than fifteen inches high. It had been placed on a crumpled dark cloth spread along the shelf. As Nile came up, she saw that the hood and cloak were coverings. There was something beneath them. She pushed the hood back with the UW's muzzle, looked at the wrinkled blackish unhuman face which might have been carved out of wood, with considerable skill. The bulging heavy-lidded eyes were closed. A narrow mouth slit was the only other feature. In its miniature ugliness it was impressive. It was as if a small demonic idol had been set up to preside over what had become of Ticos Cay's laboratory. Nile let the hood fall into place, started toward the entrance.

One more discovery then . . . she saw something stir in the dirt piled against one wall and moved the dirt aside with her foot. Three of Ticos' protohoms lay in a pile, mutilated and slashed almost beyond recognition, still moving. As cruelty it was meaningless; they had no awareness and no sensitivity to pain. But it fitted the pattern of grotesque ugliness here. The UW hissed quickly three times, taking their semblance of life from them.

There seemed no reason to stay longer. The structure held

a feeling of nightmare, heavy, almost tangible. At moments it seemed difficult to breathe and her head would begin to swim. But she had a recurrent nagging feeling of missing something. She glanced about once more. The dead shapes were there in their frozen postures. The dark little idol dreamed above them on its littered shelf. No . . . nothing else but unanswered questions.

In a thicket a hundred yards from the structure entrance, where she could watch the stretch along which she had come, Nile tried turning over the questions. Her mind moved sluggishly at first, blurred by fear and surges of pity and sick anger. She had to keep forcing all that to the back of her awareness. What she'd seen didn't fit the overall pattern she'd assumed. A very different type of mentality seemed involved. A mentality which systematically tortured human minds and bodies, leaving the victims degraded in death and carefully preserving their degradation, as if that were a goal in itself. . . .

It made no sense as yet. But the immediate situation hadn't changed. If Ticos had known about these intruders before they discovered his laboratory and converted it to the insanity in there, he might still be at large. He'd had a small boat with which he could have slipped away unnoticed to other sections of the island, or even to another island in the floatwood drift. He knew she'd be coming presently and would have tried to leave a message where she could find it, hoping she'd be able to escape capture in turn. Something to tell her what was going on, where he was.

A message where she could find it. Some place she'd associate naturally with Ticos . . . Nile shook her head. There were simply too many such places. She couldn't waste time checking them over at present. If Ticos was still in the island area, Sweeting might be able to pick up traces of him.

Her thoughts veered. The aircar. They'd have reached it by now, but door and engine keys were in the pouch at her belt. If they hadn't sunk the car or towed it away, they should still be busy around it. Watching them might tell her more about this group than she could get from Sweeting's reports. She set off quickly.

When she caught glimpses of the wind-whipped surface of the lagoon through the growth, she paused, calculating her position. The reed bed where she'd touched water should be on her right, not far away. She angled toward it, ran up a thick sloping branch stretching out above the water, turned and went on hands and knees along a lesser branch until she reached a point where sheaves of floatwood foliage overhung the lagoon. Here she straddled the branch, grasped two of the leaf stems, drew them cautiously apart and was looking down on the swirling reed tops two hundred feet below.

The area where she'd set down the car had been widened, the plants thrust aside and mashed down so that she could see a patch of open water. There were other indications that a surface craft had broken a way in from the lagoon. Nile saw nothing else, thought for a moment the car already had been destroyed or hauled off. But then she heard a series of clanging metallic sounds, partly muffled by the wind. Somebody was down there, perhaps engaged in forcing open the car's doors.

She waited, upper lip clamped between her teeth, heard no more. Then one end of the aircar edged into view, turning slowly as if it were being pushed about. A moment later all of it suddenly appeared in the open area—and on the canopy—

Nile's thoughts blurred in shock.

Parahuans. . . .

Some seventy years ago they'd come out of space to launch almost simultaneous attacks against Nandy-Cline and a dozen other water worlds of the Hub. They'd done considerable damage, but in the end their forces were pulled back; and it was believed that by the time the Federation's warships finished hunting them through space, only insignificant remnants had survived to return to their undiscovered home worlds. It had been the last open attack by an alien civilization against a Federation planet—even planets as far out from the Hub's center as Nandy-Cline.

And we became careless, Nile thought. *We felt we were so big no one would dare come again. . . .*

With a kind of frozen fascination, she stared at the two bulky amphibious creatures squatting on the car, thickly muscled legs bent sharply beneath them. A swarm of reflections based on various old descriptions of Parahuans went through her mind. The bluish-gray torsos and powerful arms were enclosed by webbings of straps, holding tools and weapons. The bulging eyes on the big round heads were double-lensed, the lower sections used for underwater vision and lidded in air, as they now were. A vocal orifice was connected to a special air system above the eyes. The two Parahuans below seemed to be gabbling at others outside her range of vision, though the wind drowned most of the sounds they were making.

Well, they had dared come again . . . and they already must be in considerable number on the unsuspecting planet, establishing themselves in and under the floatwood islands

66

in recent months. The little figure in the gutted laboratory, the small devil brooding vengefully over the mutilated husks of human bodies, was made in their image.

It changed her immediate plans. In this storm-swept multileveled mountain of dense vegetation she'd felt reasonably safe from human searchers. But she could take no chances with the aliens until she knew their capabilities. She shifted back on the branch, then halted watchfully. In the water of the lagoon beyond the reeds something was moving. Nile couldn't make out details, but it was a very large creature, dirty white in color. As she stared, it sank slowly below the surface and was gone.

She scrambled back along the branch under cover of the leaves, got to her feet as soon as she reached more solid support, and retreated hurriedly into the forest. In their first campaign the Parahuans had brought a formidable creature along with them which took part effectively in the fighting. It was animalic in behavior, though there was some evidence that it was a gigantic adaptation of the Parahuan life form. Reportedly it had sharp senses, was equally agile on land and in water, and difficult to stop with ordinary weapons.

What she'd seen out in the lagoon just now was one of those creatures—a Parahuan tarm.

Eyes shifting quickly about as she moved on, she paused here and there for an instant. Her knife reached out, slashed stem, seed pod, blossom, fleshy leaf, chunky tentacle from one or another familiar tacapu or plant form. They bled tinted dust, tinted sap, quickly turning to streaks and blots of green, shadow blue, cinnamon, chocolate brown, gray and white on Nile's body, arms, legs, face, hair, equipment. Breaking outline, blending form into background . . . a trick used in stalking floatwood species wary and keen-sighted enough to avoid undisguised human hunters.

It might not be sufficient disguise now. Humans had a variety of life detection instruments. No doubt, Parahuans had them. For many such devices, one human being in the floatwood became simply one life form blurred among many life forms. But the distinctive human scent remained, and sharp senses read it as well as instruments. She could take care of that presently. To do it, she'd have to get back to the area of Ticos' laboratory. . . .

Her mind halted a moment. Ticos' laboratory! Nile made a sound of muted fury. If he'd left a clue for her anywhere, given any time to do it, he'd left it there! She'd felt she was overlooking something. She hesitated. If she hadn't been in partial shock because of what she'd come upon—

She returned along the route she'd followed from the laboratory to the lagoon, staying some thirty feet above what should be her actual trail.

And presently: a special minor area of agitation in the mass of wind-shaken growth below and ahead. A shimmer of blue-gray.

Nile sank smoothly to the floatwood branch she was crossing, flattened herself against it, then carefully shifted position enough to let her peer down.

The Parahuan was coming out of a thicket beneath her, following another branch. He crept along on all fours. It looked awkward, but his motion was fairly rapid and showed no uncertainty. He came to a parallel bough, paused, took a short hop over to it, went on. He seemed indifferent to the fact that he was several hundred feet above the sea. So they were capable climbers. As he reached a curtain of secondary growth, another Parahuan appeared, trailing the leader by twenty-five feet, and vanished behind him. Nile checked two minutes off on her watch. No more aliens had showed up—the pair seemed to be working alone. She went up twenty feet, hurried back in the direction of the lagoon.

It had startled her that they'd been able to pick up her trail so promptly in this vast green warren. The odds seemed all against that, but there was no question that they were following it. Both carried guns, heavy-looking thick-barreled devices fastened to the web of straps about their trunks. The one in the lead had a curved box attached to the top of his head, a number of tubes projecting from its sides and twisting about in the air with a suggestion of sentient searching. The second Parahuan carried a much smaller instrument directly above the vocal slit in the upper part of his head. That probably was a communicator.

Nile dropped back down, found a place to wait. There'd been a practical detail in the information contained in the old war records: the lower half of a Parahuan's head was the best point to aim at to put them out of action quickly. Second choice was the lower torso. . . .

The leading Parahuan came into sight again on a lower branch, edging out of a wind-tossed cluster of great leaves she'd been watching. He paused there, staring about and ahead. Nile held her breath, wondering what signals he was getting from his tracking instrument, until he started forward along the branch. She let him pass below. Parahuan Number Two showed up punctually in turn. As he came within twenty-five feet, Nile sighted along the UW, squeezed the trigger carefully. The big body turned sideways, rolled off the branch without a sound.

Nile twisted left, aimed again. The leader had noticed

nothing. Moments later he too plunged down into the waving vegetation and was gone.

The buti was an unremarkable shrublike growth in the in-his category, with lacy fronds and thick woody stems, living as a semiparasite on the floatwood. Its stems were hollow, and the creamy sap they oozed when cut had the quality of nullifying a wide variety of smells, though the sap had no pronounced odor of its own. Specifically, in this case, it nullified the scents of a human body. When floatwood had been hunted over enough to make some of its harvestible life shy of human visitors, anointing oneself with buti sap, if it was obtainable, was a common move among experienced collectors.

The buti stand Nile had remembered from earlier visits was not much more than a hundred yards from Ticos' laboratory, and somewhat above it. She let herself drop thirty feet into the center of the shrubs against the antigrav effect of the belt, then spent several minutes meticulously adding a coating of the sap to her color camouflage and to the various articles of her equipment. Her nerves were on edge; she did not like at all being in the immediate vicinity of the laboratory. They might know she'd been here before —the laboratory in fact was likely to be the point where their tracking instrument had picked up the fresh human trail and started them in pursuit. There might be a swarm of the creatures not far away at the moment.

But the job with the buti couldn't be hurried too much. Nile finished it at last, cut off a two foot section of the stem, seared its ends shut with the UW and added it to the items already attached to her climb-belt. Salt water dissolved the sap; and she should have swimming to do presently. Her scent trail ended now thirty feet above the buti shrubs. If they followed it that far and could not pick it up again, they might conclude she'd lost her footing and fallen through the forest into the ocean. At any rate, she'd become as nearly indetectable as she could be.

She moved out of the stand, approached the laboratory with quick caution, conscious of a growing urgency to be out of this area. When she reached the platform, nothing seemed changed. The interior looked undisturbed; she could make out no marks of webbed Parahuan feet in the debris on the floor.

She came in quietly, gun held out before her, eyes shifting about. The rigid human exhibits watched her walk past toward Ticos' former work area. As she went by the tiny hooded idol, dreaming its dreams on the shelf, she glanced over at it.

Two thoughts flashed simultaneously into her mind.

She was in abrupt motion almost before she became fully conscious of them—spinning around toward the shelf, dropping the gun. An instant later she had whipped up both ends of the leathery cloth on which the Parahuan manikin sat, brought them together with a twist over the hooded head, gripped them hard in both hands and swept the bundled figure from the shelf.

By then there was a great deal of activity inside the cloth, a furious jerking and twisting, carried out with such amazing vigor that it nearly tore the cloth from her hands. But she swung the bundle up, slammed it down hard against the floor, brought it up, slammed it down again. The bundle stopped jerking. Nile scooped up her gun, spilled the inert thing inside the cloth out on the floor. She stood gasping and shaking in fright and hate, staring down at it.

It had shifted its position on the shelf since she'd seen it last. Not much, perhaps three or four inches. As her mind had recorded the fact, memory brought up another datum from the old records. Some rescued human prisoners had reported that the Parahuan leaders were dwarfed creatures by comparison with their fellows.

She recalled no mention of their being dwarfed to this improbable extent. But if she hadn't killed it, she might have a useful captive.

She dropped to her knees, pulled off the hood. Something attached to the thing's chest—a flat dark disk with studs in it, metallic or plastic. Attached how? Nile gripped the disk in her fingers, tugged, then slid the point of her knife in sideways between the device and the Parahuan's body, pried upward. There was a momentary resistance. Then four prongs in the underside of the instrument pulled suckingly out of the wrinkled skin. A communicator? She turned it over quickly in her hand. That was how the first trackers had known how to start on her trail. And it probably had been used again as she appeared in the entrance a minute ago, to call other searchers back to the laboratory—

She opened the kit pouch with flying fingers. There was stuff in there ordinarily used to secure some vigorously active floatwood specimen which was wanted alive—and it should hold this specimen. She pulled out flat strips of tanglecord, taped the Parahuan's small wiry arms to the dumpy body, taped the webbed feet together, sealed the narrow vocal orifice above the eyes with a section of cord. She turned the midget quickly around, looking it over for other trick devices. Nothing but a few dozen brightly colored small jewels set in the wrinkled top of the head in what might be a symbol of rank or a decorative pattern. She bundled the captive back into the cloth, knotted the ends of the cloth together, spent another dragging minute nicking the buti stem and giving the bundle the sap treatment.

She left the bundle on the floor, went over to the section of Ticos' work area and found his message to her almost at once, scrawled blandly and openly among the many notations that decorated the wall:

Nile note. The sestran stand should be carefully studied. Now out of here—fast!

She nearly, very nearly, was not fast enough. She pitched the communicator, wrapped in the midget's cloak, off the laboratory platform as she came out on it. The packaged midget himself rode her back, secured by a tanglecord harness. It was a minor nuisance; in the antigrav field his weight was nothing. . . . Less than a hundred yards from the laboratory, she ducked quietly into cover.

It was a good dense thicket. From where she crouched she could see only a limited section of the forest above. She watched that, waited for indications of anything approaching the thicket itself. A group of three Parahuans moved presently through the area above the thicket—then two more.

After that, Parahuans were simply around for a while. It was a large search party, congregating now on the laboratory. Nile kept on the move herself as much as she could, edging in the opposite direction. Most of them were climbing up from below, so she couldn't simply drop down through the forest to get out of their way. They came close enough so that she heard their voices for the first time: an oddly mellow modulated hooting, interspersed with hissing sounds. Two swarmed up the line of a grapple gun a dozen feet from her. Then she saw none for a while. By that time she had worked the green blanket of an intermediate forest canopy between herself and the main body of the searchers. She decided she was clear of them and began to climb more quickly.

Something crashed down from the upper levels ahead—a great broken branch, accompanied by assorted litter torn loose in its descent. Nile looked up, and her mind went bright with terror. She took one slow step to the side, thumbed the antigrav up high. Nothing beneath her feet now . . . she was falling limply, bonelessly, turning over slowly, toward the shelter of the canopy below. No human motions. No voluntary motions of any kind. Be a leaf, an undefinably colored uninteresting small dead dropping part of the forest. She reached the canopy, settled through it, went drifting down until she touched a solid branch and motion stopped. She huddled there, clutching the growth on either side of her. Fear still stormed along her nerves.

The tarm had been like the tip of a fog bank swirling into sight around a floatwood bole above her. It was rushing by overhead as she dropped, so close that it seemed almost impossible she'd remained unnoticed—close enough, she thought, for one of its pale tentacles to have reached down and plucked her from the air. But it had moved on. She listened to the receding sounds of its passage through the forest long enough to make sure it wasn't returning, then set off hastily, still shaking. She wasn't nearly as far from the laboratory as she should be before the search fanned out again. They must have discovered by now that their midget was missing. Nile told herself they were least likely to come back to an area already hunted over by the tarm.

She might have been right. Ten minutes passed without further signs of her pursuers, and her nerves steadied again.

If they'd shifted to the eastern areas of the forest, it could keep them futilely occupied until nightfall. Flashes of fading sunlight began to reach her. She wasn't far now from the forest roof on the seaward side and should not be far either from the sestran stand to which Ticos Cay's note had directed her. Eight months before, they'd brought sestran shoots from another part of the island and established them here for his studies. He'd known his use of the term would tell her exactly where to look.

She discovered the stand presently—and discovered also that chaquoteels had built a colony nest above it since she'd been here last. The tiny kesters greeted her with a storm of furious whistlings. Nile ducked quickly into the sestran, but not quickly enough. The chaquoteels were on her in a darting rainbow swarm, and her back smarted from dozens of jabs before they decided she'd been sufficiently routed and left her alone in the vegetation. Then the racket quieted quickly again.

Her search was a short one; Ticos had done what she'd expected. The tiny script recorder was in weatherproof sealing, taped to the side of one of the thickest sestran stems. Nile freed herself of her prisoner and laid the bundle down where she could watch it. The midget hadn't stirred yet, but that didn't mean he wasn't awake.

She considered briefly. There was cover all about. If Parahuans, or the tarm, showed up, she could fade away in any direction without stepping into the open. And with a few hundred bad-tempered chaquoteels scattered around the vicinity, she couldn't be taken by surprise.

Yes—as good a place as any to find out what Ticos had to tell her. . . .

Nile settled down, fitted the recorder to her eye, and started it.

5

Long before she put the recorder down for the last time, Nile had decided that Ticos Cay ranked among the great liars of history.

He was still alive. At least he'd been alive less than a week ago when he left the last of the four recorder disks which contained his report here for her.

She sat still, sorting over the information.

Some seventy years ago the Parahuan leadership had been smarting in defeat and trying to understand how defeat could have been possible. In their minds they were the race which had achieved perfection at all levels, including individual immortality for those with the greatness to attain it. They were the Everliving. None could match them. The water worlds of the galaxy which met their requirements were destined to be their own.

Since they first moved out from Porad Anz, their home world, the Sacred Sea, they had encountered nothing to contradict that assumption.

But now an inferior land-dweller which was in possession of a number of such worlds had flung back and almost completely destroyed the Parahuan forces sent to occupy them. The experience stunned the Everliving. It affronted logic.

Before the attack they had made what seemed a sufficiently comprehensive study of the Federation of the Hub. This human civilization was huge. But it was a heterogeneous, loosely organized, loosely governed mass of individuals quite normally in serious conflict among themselves. The analysis of captured humans confirmed the picture.

That muddled, erratic, emotionally swayed creature had routed the disciplined Parahuan forces. Something was wrong —it simply shouldn't have happened.

What had been overlooked?

They went back to studying the enemy in every way they could. The creature was blocking the orderly procession of the goals of Porad Anz. That was intolerable. The secret of its ability to do it must be found—and then means devised to destroy the ability.

Presently, in the creature's relatively recent history, a clue was discovered.

It developed into the Tuvela Theory. . . .

Nile made a snorting, incredulous sound. Not much more than two centuries ago—not many decades before Ticos Cay was born—the Hub still had been one of the bloodiest human battlegrounds of all time. It was the tail end of the War Centuries. A thousand governments were forming and breaking interstellar alliances, aiming for control of the central clusters or struggling to keep from being overwhelmed.

The Tuvelas belonged in the later part of that pre-Federation period. They were a sophisticated equivalent of ancient warlords. Some believed they arose from well-defined genetic strains at a high genius level. Legends clustered about their activities. But the fact was that the records of those muddled times were contradictory and thoroughly unreliable. In any event, the Tuvelas were long gone.

The Parahuan Palachs, searching for an explanation of their own defeat, decided they weren't long gone. The mys-

terious superhuman Tuvelas not only were still around—
they were now the true secret rulers of the Federation of
the Hub. They had organized and guided the operations
which resulted in the defeat of the Parahuan expeditionary
forces.

The Everliving, or at least a majority of them, didn't intend to let the matter rest there. They now had a rationali-
zation of the past disaster, and it restored to some extent
their shattered pride. To have been bested by a foe of abnormal ability whose existence hadn't been suspected, that
could be accepted. The human species as such was inferior
to Porad Anz. Its apparent strength lay in the fact that its
vast masses were directed and controlled by these freakish
monsters.

To even the score with the Tuvelas, to bring them down
and destroy them, became an abiding obsession with the
Everliving—or again, at least with a majority of them. Some
evidently felt from the beginning that the Tuvelas might be
such dangerous opponents that it would be better not to
come into conflict with them a second time. The view never
became popular, but it was agreed that all reasonable precautions should be taken to avoid another debacle. The
majority opinion remained that since a Parahuan Great Palach was the ultimate development of life, the human Tuvela
could not possibly be his superior. The advantage of the
Tuvelas had been solely that the Everliving hadn't known
they were there—and naturally hadn't considered such a remote possibility in preparing the first attack.

Out of this situation grew the Great Plan, aimed at the
ultimate destruction of the Hub's rulers and of the Hub as a
civilization. The conflicting opinions were represented by
the groups known as the Voice of Action and the Voice of

Caution. Between these opposed factions, the uncommitted ranks of the Everliving maintained the wisely flexible Balance.

The Voice of Caution had determinedly dragged its heels from the start and continued to drag them for seventy years. In spite of such resistance, the Great Plan gradually matured. The Parahuans found allies—the Hub had more enemies with long memories among the stars than it might know. But they were wary enemies. If the Parahuans could take and hold a number of Federation worlds and engage a major portion of the Federation's forces . . . *then* a score of alien civilizations would attack other points in the Hub simultaneously, splitting and weakening the human defenses until they were shattered. But only if the Parahuans succeeded.

The Voice of Action argued that this was good enough. The Voice of Caution argued that it wasn't. In the Balance between them an initial test was decreed—a potential invasion force was maneuvered with careful secrecy into the seas of Nandy-Cline.

This force was regarded as expendable. On the face of it, it should be able to take Nandy-Cline with relative ease in a coordinated surprise attack. Careful study had established the fact beyond a doubt. But its primary purpose was to flush the Tuvelas to view and test their alertness and ability. If it should be established that they were indeed entities against whom the Everliving were outmatched—if, for example, the invasion force, in spite of its apparent superiority, again was destroyed or obliged to retreat, the most disconcerting aspects of the Tuvela Theory must be considered proved. Then the Great Plan would be canceled and Porad Anz would resign itself to a future of circumspect obscurity.

But if Nandy-Cline fell as scheduled, the Tuvelas could

be dealt with, now that their influence on humanity was known; and the Voice of Action would receive full authority to proceed with the further operations designed to end in the destruction of the Hub.

In the course of preparing for the attack on the planet, the hidden invasion force ran head-on into Dr. Ticos Cay. . . .

Ticos had been tracked to his laboratory and taken by surprise. A study of the lab's equipment told his captors that here was a human with advanced scientific knowledge who might have useful information. He was treated with care, questioned at length. Many Palachs had acquired a faultless command of translingue as an aid to their understanding of the enemy. They interrogated Ticos under drugs and with the application of calculated pain. His acquired level of mental control enabled him to withstand such pressures; and the Palachs considered this to be of great interest. No other human prisoner had shown a similar ability.

They were further intrigued to discover he had been working, among other things, at the development of longevity drugs. All reports indicated that humans had never attained an unlimited life span; the lack of an overall immortality program was in fact the most definite indication that the Hub's civilization, in spite of its accomplishments in other fields, stood basically at a low level. Among themselves, the science of immortality in all its branches was held sacred, its study restricted to Palachs. Evidently it was at this point they decided Ticos might belong to a class of humanity which knew at least something about the Tuvelas. Earlier prisoners had been totally ignorant even of the existence of their anonymous rulers.

Ticos was puzzled at first by the new direction the interrogations were taking. He framed his replies very carefully in a manner designed to draw more revealing questions. Presently his concept of the Palachs' Tuvela Theory grew clear— and now he was able to suggest possibilities which seemed to confirm the worst fears of his inquisitors. He could claim convincingly that the specific information he had was quite limited, but the implications in what he said matched to a disturbing degree the blackest calculations made concerning the nature of Tuvelas. The majority of the Everliving connected with the expeditionary force found their faith in themselves again shaken. Endless bitter debates were unleashed between the opposed groups, while the Balance, temporarily at least, shifted toward the views of the Voice of Caution. The invasion was not actually called off, but all immediate attack plans were stalled for the time being.

Ticos meanwhile had been in an anxious quandary of his own. Nile's next scheduled visit was some weeks away; but she was bound to come then, and that he would have been able to persuade the Palachs to abandon the planet before she arrived seemed hardly possible. If he did nothing, she either would be killed out of hand as she came down from the air or captured and put to death in some very unpleasant manner. The Parahuans were not at all gentle with ordinary prisoners. As far as he knew, he was the only one picked up on Nandy-Cline who had lived more than a few days in their hands.

So he'd turned Nile into a Tuvela. It made one thing certain: the Palachs wouldn't kill her while they saw a chance of taking her alive—and knowing Nile as he did he felt that might very well give her an opportunity to escape into the forests. Parahuan scientists were studying the results of his longevity experiments; and he was allowed to go about the floatwood under guard at regular intervals to collect the materials he wanted. On such occasions he would deposit the significant information he had gathered where she should find it. After reading this report, she should do what she could to get away from the island and alert the planet. However, if she was captured, they might still be able to maintain the Tuvela bluff together and bring about a withdrawal of the alien forces. Success was questionable; but it was the best course he could suggest. . . .

Nile inhaled shakily, blinking at the knotted cloth containing a Parahuan Palach. A *Great* Palach, she corrected herself. She'd better have her information well memorized in case events made it necessary to attempt to play the role of Tuvela Ticos had bestowed on her. Going by the descriptions he'd given of his principal interrogators, she thought she could even call this particular Great Palach by name.

She pursed her lips, thinking it over. She already had plans for escaping from the island presently, with Danrich Parrol's help. But the plans didn't make provision as yet for getting Ticos out, and she didn't intend to leave without him.

Besides, the general situation had evidently become one which could take an unpredictable turn at any time. The Everliving, already sufficiently overwrought as a result of Ticos' machinations, had tipped their hand in trying to take her alive and failing to do it. If they suspected she could get away from the island again and warn Nandy-Cline, it might stampede them into launching the overall attack immediately, before they lost the advantage of surprise. At best that would cost a great many human lives. . . .

Lives that would be saved if the aliens could be talked into withdrawing.

Nile's reflections checked there a moment. She didn't like the line they were taking—but the line was an inevitable one. As things had worked out, the Palachs had reason to believe that in her they were dealing with a genuine Tuvela. If Ticos had come close to persuading them to retreat from the planet, a genuine Tuvela should be able to finish the job.

But that meant putting herself voluntarily in the power of those creatures. And the thought was enough to dry her mouth. . . .

A chaquoteel whistled a dozen feet away, and Nile started violently, then cursed her jittering nerves. It hadn't been an alarm call. Nothing of significance to the chaquoteels, and therefore to her, had come near the sestran stand since she'd been sitting here.

She looked at the bundled Great Palach again. He was awake. There'd been occasional cautious stirrings under the cloth. One question was simply whether she could play the part of a Tuvela-Guardian well enough to keep the aliens deceived. The midget in there was a highly aggressive representative of the Voice of Action. If she could sell *him* the idea that Porad Anz was doomed if it persisted in challenging the Tuvelas, there was a good chance she could bluff the Everliving as a whole.

Why not find out?

She'd have to believe it herself first. Quit being Nile Etland and *be* a Tuvela. The more outrageously, the better. No small lies—big ones. Keep the creature surprised.

She moistened her lips, fished the tanglecord's release key from her pouch, placed her gun on the chunk of floatwood supporting the thicket. The tanglecord strips securing the cloth about the Parahuan came away at the touch of the key. She dropped them in the pouch, unknotted the cloth and drew it cautiously from the captive.

The atmosphere sections of the Parahuan's eyes were open. They watched her steadily. The tanglecord clamped about his arms and feet was tight and in place. Nile pulled the strip away from the vocal slit, set him upright against a clump of sestran, backed away eight or nine feet, and sat down, holding the gun loosely before her. She studied the alien for some seconds.

He didn't look too formidable, but Ticos' caution against underestimating Palachs of any grade probably was well founded. Their approach to immortality involved a progressive induced metamorphosis. The muscular structure became condensed and acquired extreme efficiency. Most of the thinking apparatus was buried inside the chunky torso; presumably it did not undergo physiological changes. Reduced to essentials, Ticos had said. Very well, she'd watch this Great Palach. . . .

What did he see in her? A Tuvela? Nile had a mental picture of herself—lean, next to naked, smeared with colorful plant sap. Hardly the most impressive image. But it couldn't be helped. She was a Guardian of the Federation of the Hub, a Tuvela. To him, she was gromgorru. A mysterious, powerful being, with information sources beyond her captive's knowledge. The last, at any rate, she had.

She said, "I believe I am addressing the Great Palach Koll."

The manikin stared a long moment. At last the vocal slit moved. "And *I* believe," a voice like golden velvet told her, "that I address a Hulon named Etland."

Hulon—Parahuan term signifying low-grade human.

There'd been no suggestion of alien inflection in the words. They *had* studied humanity in patient detail.

"You have another name for us," the Tuvela said indifferently. "Call me Hulon if you wish. Where are you holding Dr. Cay at present?"

"Not far from here. What is your interest in Dr. Cay?"

"Our interest in Dr. Cay," Nile said, "is less than it was. He has not performed well in this test."

"Test?" Koll's voice had thinned. Nile regarded him a moment.

"Surely you must have wondered from time to time," she remarked, "why no one came here to inspect Dr. Cay's activities. Yes, a test. Not that it's your concern, Great Palach, but Dr. Cay was a candidate for the true-life. I'm not sure he will remain one. When we saw you had discovered him, we waited to observe how capably he would handle this unexpected situation. I'm disappointed in him."

Koll's vocal slit opened and closed silently twice. The Tuvela scowled absently.

"However, I'm more than disappointed in the Everliving," she resumed. "If you didn't find Dr. Cay sufficiently persuasive, very moderate intelligence alone should have told you to be long gone from here . . . and glad to be away! Haven't you felt the snare this world represents waiting about you? Has the Sacred Sea grown senile instead of immortal?"

She shrugged. A Tuvela, after all, was not greatly interested in the limitations of Porad Anz.

"You'll be told to go now," she stated. "You've been butchering the ones you call Hulons a little too freely. That disgusts me. It seems you fear even the human shape so much you revert to your animal beginnings when you meet it. We don't choose to see our people wasted—and Dr. Cay has had time enough to demonstrate his present lack of satisfactory potential."

Silence. Long silence. The sestran shrubs rustled. Wind roaring rose and ebbed in the distance. The air was darkening quickly. The wizened manikin sat motionless, staring.

Gromgorru, Nile thought. It had been weighing on both sides. It should weigh heavily on the Parahuans now. A Tuvela was about, an invisible ghost in the floatwood. It had plucked the Great Palach Koll from his grisly command post. Bear down on those fears. Yes, it might very well work. . . .

The velvet voice said suddenly, "I see and hear a creature lying in clever desperation to conceal its helplessness. You can't escape and you can't contact your kind. You did not come here to tell the Everliving they must leave. You're here because you were trapped."

Nile's lips curled. "The sken beam? If the technicians who examined my car understood what they saw, they must know I could have blocked such a device. And by the true-life, I believe I can play the hunting game against a mob of Oganoon and stupid animals! Great Palach Koll, Voice of Action—look around! Who is trapped here, and who is helpless?"

She leaned forward. "The stupidity of Porad Anz! It tampered with our worlds and was thrown out. All it learned was to look for allies before it tried to come back. No doubt you'd need allies—more than you can find. But you've already found too many to make the Great Plan possible! Even if we'd had no other methods of information, your secret was spread too far to remain a secret—"

She broke off. Koll was quivering. The vocal slit made spitting sounds.

"We'd been minded to spare you," the Tuvela began again. "But—"

"Guardian, be silent!" The voice was squeezed down to an angry whine. "Lies and tricks! The Everliving will not listen!"

The Tuvela laughed. "When I come to them with a Great Palach tied in a rag, dangling headdown from my belt, they won't listen?"

Koll squealed—and became a blur of rubbery motion. The long legs swung up, brought the fettered feet to his shoulder. Something projected in that instant from the shoulder, a half-inch jet of fire. It touched the tanglecord, and the tanglecord parted. The webbed toes of one foot gripped one of the jewels on Koll's head, pulled it free. The other leg was beneath him again; it bent, straightened; and he came toward Nile in a long, one-legged hop, quick and balanced. The jewel-handled needle gripped in his foot leveled out. . . .

Nile was in motion herself by then, dropping back, rolling sideways—

The needle spat a thread of pink radiance along her flank as she triggered the UW.

And that was that. The UW's beam was hot, and Koll was in mid-jump, moving fast, as it caught him. His lumpy torso was very nearly cut in two.

Nile got up shakily, parted the sestran stems through which he had plunged, and looked down from the floatwood branch. Nothing but the waving, shadowy greenery of the vertical jungle below . . . and no point in hunting around for the body of the Great Palach down there. Ticos had neglected to mention that the thick Parahuan hide could be used to conceal an arsenal, but after seeing the communicator Koll carried grafted to himself, the possibility should have occurred to her.

Why had he attacked at that particular moment? She hadn't convinced him Porad Anz faced destruction unless the invading force withdrew—or else he had such a seething hatred for mankind that the fate of his own race was no longer of sufficient consideration. But apparently she *had* convinced him that a majority of the Palachs would accept what she said.

He should know, Nile thought. She'd lost her prisoner, but the Great Palach Koll dead, silenced, vanished, remained an impressive witness to the Tuvelas' capability and stern ruthlessness.

Let the Everliving stew in the situation a while. She'd give them indications presently that she was still around the island. That should check any impulse to launch a hasty military operation. Meanwhile she'd try to find out where Ticos was held, and prepare to carry out other plans . . . And now it was time to check with Sweeting and learn what her water scouting had revealed.

Nile dropped quietly down out of the sestran thicket to lower branches to avoid arousing the chaquoteels, and slipped away into the forest.

Back down at the water's edge, she looked out from a niche between two trunks at the neighboring island section. It was the largest of the five connected forests, a good half wider and longer than this one and lifting at least a hundred yards farther into the air. From the car she'd seen thick clusters of a dark leafless growth rising higher still from a point near the forest's center, like slender flexible spear shafts whipping in the wind. Oilwood it was called. Weeks from now, when the island rode into the electric storm belts of the polar sea, the oilwood would draw lightning from the sky to let its combustible sheathing burn away and the ripened seeds beneath tumble down through the forest into the ocean.

Set ablaze deliberately tonight, it should provide a beacon to mark the island for Parrol and let him know where she was to be found.

The water between the two forests wasn't open. The submerged root system extended from one to the other; and on the roots grew the floatwood's aquatic symbiotes, pushing out from the central lagoon, though their ranks thinned as they approached the rush of the open sea. The Parahuans wouldn't have stopped hunting for her, and ambushes could easily be laid in that area. The sea south of the forest seemed to offer a safer crossing, now that evening darkened the sky and reduced surface visibility. The Meral Current carried weed beds: dense moving jungles which provided cover when needed.

Nile gave the otter caller on her wrist another turn. Sweeting should be here quickly. A receiver embedded in her skull transmitted the signals to her brain, and she homed in unerringly on the caller.

"Nile—"

"Over here, Sweeting!"

Sweeting came up out of the water twenty feet away, shook herself vigorously, rippled along the side of the floatwood bole and settled beside Nile.

"These are *new* bad guys!" she stated.

"Yes," said Nile. "New and bad. They don't belong on our world. What can you tell me about them?"

"Much," Sweeting assured her. "But found two Nile-friends. They tell you more."

"Two—" Nile broke off. In the surging sea five yards below, two dark whiskered heads had appeared on the surface, were looking up at her.

Wild otters.

6

THE WILD OTTERS were a mated pair who'd selected the floatwood lagoon as their private preserve. The male would nearly match Spiff in size. The female was young, a smaller edition of Sweeting. They might be three or four generations away from domestication, but they used translingue as readily as Sweeting and much in her style. Interspersed were unfamiliar terms based on their independent oceanic existence, expressing matters for which no human words had been available. Usually Nile could make out their sense.

When the Parahuans arrived, the curious otters had made a game of studying the unfamiliar creatures and their gadgetry. There was a ship anchored to the island under the floor of the lagoon. It was considerably bigger than the average human submersible, chunky and heavily built—evidently a spaceship. Its lock was always open on the water. A second ship, a huge one, was also in the vicinity. Normally it stayed deep in the sea, but at times it had moved up almost to the island. Ticos had said that the headquarters ship of the Parahuan expedition seemed to be accompanying this floatwood drift.

Above sea level the Parahuans had set up ten or twelve posts in the forest. Most of them were small, probably observation points or weapon emplacements. The exception was in the island section to which Nile wanted to go. "Big house," Sweeting said. It was set near the edge of the lagoon, extending well back into the floatwood and completely concealed by it. Perhaps a fifth of the structure was under water. Nile got the impression of something like a large blockhouse or fort, a few hundred yards beyond the rookery of the sea-havals. She wouldn't have selected the giant kesters as neighbors herself—the rookery was an evil-smelling and very noisy place—but alien senses might not find that disturbing.

The immediately important thing about the blockhouse was that it told her exactly where Ticos could be found, unless he'd been taken away after her arrival. He'd said his captors had shifted him and his equipment to such a structure and described its location.

The wild otters knew nothing of Ticos, but they did know about the tarm. When the Parahuans first came, there'd been two of the pale monsters in the lagoon from time to time. One of them evidently had been taken away again shortly afterward. The description they gave of the other one matched that of the records. It was an aggressive beast which fed heavily on sea life and made occasional forays into upper forest levels.

"Have you had any trouble with it?" Nile asked.

The question seemed to surprise them. Then they gave her the silent otter laugh, jaws open.

"No trouble. Tarm's *slow!*" Sweeting's small kinswoman explained.

"Slow for you," Nile said. Hunting otters had their own notions about water speed. "Could I keep away from it in the water?"

They considered.

"Jets, heh?" the big male asked.

"Sadly, no jets!" Sweeting made a stroking motion with

her forelegs, flipped hind feet up briefly. "Human swim. . . ."

"Human swim! Tarm thing eat you!" the female told Nile decisively. "You hide, keep no-smell, Nile! How do the no-smell? Trick, heh?"

"Uh-huh. A trick. But it won't work in the water."

The male grunted reflectively. "Tarm's back under big house. Might stay, might not." He addressed the female. "Best poison-kill it soon?"

Poison-killing, it developed, involved a contraption put together of drift weed materials—hollow reeds and thorns chewed to fit the hollows and smeared with exceedingly poisonous yellow bladder gum. Wild otter tribes had developed the device to bring down flying kesters for a change of diet. The female demonstrated, rolling over on her back, holding an imaginary hole-stock to her mouth and making a popping noise through her lips. "Splash come kester!" They'd modified the technique to handle the occasional large predators who annoyed them too persistently —larger thorns, jammed directly through the hide into the body. Big sea animals didn't die as quickly as the fliers, but they died.

"Many thorns here," the male assured Nile. "Stick in ten, twenty, and the tarm no trouble."

She studied him thoughtfully. Sweeting could count . . . but these were wild otters. Attempts had been made to trace the original consignment of laboratory-grown cubs to its source. But the trail soon became hopelessly lost in the giant intricacies of Hub commerce; and no laboratory was found which would take responsibility for the development of a talking otter mutant. The cubs which had reached

Nandy-Cline seemed to be the only members of the strain in existence.

For all practical purposes then, this was a new species, and evidently it was less than fifty years old. In that time it had progressed to the point of inventing workable dart blowguns and poisoned daggers. It might have an interesting future. Nile thought she knew the yellow bladder gum to which they referred. It contained a very fast acting nerve poison. What effect it would have on a creature with the tarm's metabolism couldn't be predicted, but the idea seemed worth trying.

She asked further questions, gathered they'd seen the tarm motionless under the blockhouse only minutes before Sweeting got the first caller signal. It was the creature's usual station as water guard of the area. Evidently it had been withdrawn from the hunt for the Tuvela. Groups of Parahuans were moving about in the lagoon, but there was no indication they were deployed in specific search patterns. . . .

"Waddle-feet got jets," remarked the male.

"Slow jets," said the female reassuringly. "No trouble!"

But armed divers in any kind of jet rigs could be trouble in open water. Nile shrugged mentally. She could risk the crossing. She nodded at the dark outlines of the distant forest section.

"I've got to go over there," she said. "Sweeting will come along. The waddle-feet have guns and are looking for me. You want to come too?"

They gave her the silent laugh again, curved white teeth gleaming in the dusk.

"Nile-friends," stated the male. "We'll come. Fun, heh? What we do, Nile? Kill the waddle-feet?"

"If we run into any of them," said Nile, "we kill the waddle-feet fast!"

A few minutes later the three otters slipped down into a lifting wave and were gone. Nile glanced about once more before following. A narrow sun-rim still clung to the horizon. Overhead the sky was clear—pale blue with ghostly cluster light shining whitely through. High-riding cloud banks to the south reflected magenta sun glow. Wind force was moderate. Here in the lee of the forest she didn't feel much of it. The open stretch of sea ahead was broken and foaming, but she'd be moving below the commotion.

In these latitudes the Meral produced its own surface illumination. She saw occasional gleams flash and disappear among the tossing waves—colonies of light organisms responding to the darkening air. But they wouldn't give enough light to guide her across. Time to shift to her night eyes. . . .

She brought a pack of dark-lenses from the pouch, fitted two under her lids, blinked them into position: a gel, adjusting itself automatically to varying conditions for optimum human vision. An experimental Giard product, and a very good one.

She pulled the breather over her face, fitted the audio plugs to her ears, and flicked herself off the floatwood. Sea shadow closed about her, cleared in seconds to amber half-light as the dark-lenses went into action. Fifteen feet down, Nile turned and stroked into open water.

Open but not empty. A moving weed thicket ahead and to the right . . . Nile circled about it, a school of small skilts darting past, brushing her legs with tiny hard flicks. She brought her left wrist briefly before her eyes, checked the small compass she'd fastened to it, making sure of her direction. The otters weren't in view. If the crossing was uneventful, she shouldn't see much of them. They were to stay about a hundred feet away, one of the wild pair on either side, Sweeting taking the point, to provide early warning of approaching danger.

A cloud of light appeared presently ahead; others grew dimly visible beyond it . . . pink, green, orange. The Shining Sea was the name the sledmen gave the Meral as it rolled here down the southern curve of the globe toward the pole. Nile began to pass thickets in which the light-bearers clustered. Each species produced its own precise shade of waterfire. None were large; the giants among them might be half the length of her forearm, narrow worm bodies. But their swarms turned acres of the subsurface to flame.

The fins moved her on steadily. She listened to the sea through the audios, sensed its changing vibrations against her skin. Amber dimness of open water for a while; then she went turning and twisting through a soggy dark forest of weed. Beyond it, light glowed again. She avoided the brightest areas—too easy to be spotted there.

Sweeting came to her once, circled about, was gone, a flicking shadow. Not an alarm report; the otter had checked on her position.

Then there was a sound which momentarily overrode the myriad other sounds of the Meral. A deep, distant booming. Half a minute later it was repeated. Closer now.

Nile held her course but moved toward the surface, scanning the areas below and ahead of her. The giant sea-havals were hunting. An encounter with one of the great creatures in the open sea ordinarily brought no risk to a human swimmer or, in fact, to anything but a sizable skilt. Sea-havals hunted by scent and sight; and skilts were their only prey. But when they made *that* sound, they were driving a major school. To avoid accidents, it was best to keep well out of the way of such a school. . . .

If possible, Nile added mentally.

And there came the first indications of trouble!

A dozen big torpedo shapes hurtled toward her, coming from a line of light-thickets ahead. Skilts—approximately in the three hundred pound class. Preferred size for a sea-haval.

Nile checked, moved quickly to the side, lifted farther toward the surface . . . near enough to feel the tugging surge of the swells—

The sea boomed like the stroke of a tremendous bell.

And the string of light-thickets exploded as the van of the skilt school bulleted through them. Coming at her in a straight line. They were harmless creatures in themselves, but their panic, speed and weight made them deadly now. The impact of any of them would break her body apart. And the sea seemed an onrushing mass of thousands.

The scene was blotted from Nile's vision as she broke the surface. She rolled herself into a tight ball. There was nothing else she could do. A great wave lifted her. Then came a vast, thudding sensation from below, streaming past, a racing river which threatened to drag her down. Skilts exploded from the sea in frantic thirty foot leaps all about, came smashing back to the surface. Then two final tremendous surges of the water beneath her. A pair of sea-havals had gone past.

Sweeting was there an instant later. The wild otters arrived almost as promptly.

"Nile here, heh? . . . Fun, heh?"

Nile had no comments. She'd pulled off the breather, was gulping long lungfuls of storm air. Dim and remote, more sensed by her nerves than heard, came an echo of the sea-havals' booming. The hunt had moved on.

Moments later, she and the otters were underway again. For the next two hundred yards, weed beds were ripped and shredded by the passage of the fleeing school. Cleanly sectioned skilts, chopped by the big kesters, drifted about. Then things began to look normal. . . .

Suddenly Sweeting was back, moving past Nile's face in a swirl of water, dropping a dozen feet, checking to turn, turning again and gliding toward a great limp tangle of weeds below her. Nile followed instantly in a spurt of speed. *Come fast!* was what that had meant.

She slipped into the rubbery slickness of the thicket. The otter was there, waiting. Far enough, apparently. . . . Nile turned, took out the UW, parted the weeds enough to see anything coming toward her. When she glanced aside again, Sweeting was gone.

She waited. A light-thicket hung twenty yards to her left; about her was dimness. Small skilt shadows slipped past, and something big and chunky drifted up, slowly turning head-on as it came opposite her to stare in at her among the weeds. It paused, moved off. A large weed skilt, perhaps three times the weight of the maddened projectiles which had made up the school. A carrion eater by preference. It should do well in the wake of the sea-havals' hunt tonight—

Abrupt violent commotion—swirling of water, lifting and sinking of the weed fronds, thudding sensations which suddenly stopped. . . . Nile knew the pattern of an underwater death fight; and this had been one, not many yards away.

It was over now. She slipped forward, gun held out, peering up. Dark smoky veils floated down and something bulky came settling through them, grazing the weed tangle. The Parahuan's head seemed nearly detached from the squat body, blood pumping out through the throat gashes. Typical otter work.

Sweeting reappeared from above. Together they hauled the unwieldy thing by its harness straps into the weeds. Fastened to the broad back was the Parahuan version of a jet rig. Nile studied it a moment, gave up the notion of converting the device to her own use; she would lose more time over that than it should take her to get back into the floatwood. They left the big rubbery body wedged in the center of the tangle. As they turned away, the first scavenging weed skilt was nosing up toward it from the other side.

A hissing had begun in the audio pickup and was growing louder. Nile halted Sweeting in the trailing fringes of the thicket. Then two other bulky figures were slanting down swiftly through open water toward them, trailed by thin jet tracks. The Parahuans' guns were in their hands. Possibly they had picked up traces of the brief commotion and were looking for their dead companion. At any rate, they were hardly twenty-five feet away when Nile saw them, and their faces were turned toward her, semicircular water eyes staring. The UW couldn't miss on such targets, and didn't.

The immediate vicinity of a sea-haval rookery at night was not for the nervous. Monstrous rumblings and splashings came from within the floatwood walls surrounding it, as the adult kesters left the rookery by a diving hole hacked through the forest's subsurface root floor, returned presently, beakspears holding up to a ton of mangled skilts, to be greeted by the roars of their gigantic young.

Upwind of the racket, on the lagoon side, Nile finished recoating herself and her equipment with buti sap. She was down among the massive boles near the water, waiting for Sweeting to return and report. While they were dealing with three members of the Parahuan sea patrol, the wild otters had found and dispatched another three. That seemed to have left no survivors. But the patrol should have been missed by now; and what she did next would depend at least in part on what the Parahuans were doing as a result.

The tarm had been found still at its station beneath the blockhouse. Nile was thankful for that. The sudden near-encounter in the other forest with the pallid sea thing had rammed fear deep into her nerves; the thought of it hadn't been far from her mind since. The early reports that the Parahuans might have developed the monsters out of their own kind somehow made the tarm more horrible. After seeing what their biological skills had done in creating the form of a Great Palach, Nile thought it was possible. She told herself the buti and reasonable caution would keep the creature from noticing her if she met it again, but she wasn't at all sure of that. And the buti would be no protection if it came near her in the water.

Her wild allies might presently free her of that particular fear. They'd gone to get a supply of the poisoned thorns and seemed confident that in the underwater tangle of float-wood beneath the blockhouse they could plant a lethal dose into the tarm's huge body without too much trouble. Sweeting was prowling the lagoon, looking for signs of alien activity there or in the forest near Nile.

"Found Tikkos, Nile!"

"Where?"

Sweeting slipped up along the bough out of the lagoon, crouched beside her. "In boat," she said. "With little waddle-feet."

"*Little* waddle-feet?" Palachs?

"Half-size," said Sweeting. "Five, six. Tikkos talking to Guardian Etland. Then waddle-feet talking to Guardian Etland. Loud-voice. You Guardian Etland, heh?"

"The waddle-feet think so." Loud-voice was a loudspeaking device. "Let's get this straight! First, where's the boat Ticos and the waddle-feet are in?"

The otter's nose indicated the eastern end of the forest. "Boat's coming into lagoon. Coming this way. Got lights. Got loud-voice. Talking to forest. They think Guardian Etland's in forest. Tikkos say waddle-feet talk, not fight. You talk and maybe they go away. Waddle-feet say they sorry about fighting. No guns in boat. You come talk, please." Sweeting paused, watching her. "Kill them, get Tikkos now, heh?"

"No," Nile said. "No, we don't kill them. I'd better hear what they have to say. You say the boat's coming in this direction—"

"Coming slow. You don't listen to waddle-feet, Nile! Trick, heh? You come close, they kill you."

"It may not be a trick. Stay here."

But she felt shaky as she climbed quickly back into the forest toward the sea-haval rookery. The theoretical Tuvela, totally self-confident, certainly would be willing to talk to the aliens at this point, press the psychological advantage she'd gained. On the other hand, the Tuvela presumably would know what to do if it turned out she'd stepped into a Parahuan trap. Nile wasn't sure she would know what to do.

She caught her breath briefly as the wind backed up and assorted rookery stenches billowed around her. Far enough from the lagoon. . . . She opened the pouch, took out the roll of tanglecord, added the otter caller to the other items, closed the pouch and shoved it into one of the fins, the buti stick into the other. She taped the fins together. They made a compact package which she wedged into a float-wood niche and secured further with tanglecord, leaving the roll stuck to the package. She was keeping the climb-belt and the UW.

She looked around a moment, memorizing the place, started back to the lagoon. Sweeting was hissing with alarm and disapproval when she got there. Nile calmed the otter, explained the situation as well as she could. The boat lights hadn't yet appeared around the curve of the forest to the east. They set off in that direction, Nile moving through the floatwood not far from the edge of the lagoon, Sweeting in the water slightly ahead of her. If a trap had been laid, they should spot it between them before they were in it. . . .

Going by Ticos' descriptions, the six Parahuans in the boat with him were Palachs. Concealed at a point some fifty feet above the water, Nile looked them over. Two were about his size; four ranged down from there, though none came near the midget level. In the boat lights they displayed odd headgears and elaborate harness arrangements . . . and, of course, they might be carrying concealed weapons.

She studied Ticos more carefully than his companions.

There was a stiffness in the way he moved which showed he wasn't in good physical condition. But his amplified voice was clear; and if his phrasing had more than a suggestion of obsequiousness about it, that fitted the role he was playing: an inferior addressing the Guardian. A role of his own choosing; not one he had been forced to assume.

She was convinced that so far there was no trap. But there were other considerations. . . .

The loudspeaker began booming about her again. It was set to penetrate high and deep into the forest, overriding the surging winds, to reach the attention of the Guardian Etland wherever she might be. Ticos and one of the Palachs used it alternately. The others squatted about the boat as it moved slowly through the lagoon along the forest.

The message was repetitious. She'd been listening to it for the past few minutes, keeping pace with the boat. Her talk with the Great Palach Koll had been monitored by the Everliving. The transmitting device presumably had been another of the jewels fixed to Koll's head; and the idea might have been Koll's—to let the other Great Palachs and Palachs follow his interrogation of the captured human, witness the collapse of her pretensions as Guardian and Tuvela. If so, the plan had backfired. Everything said, the fact that Koll was the prisoner, the Tuvela's evident knowledge of Porad Anz's secrets, was designed to further undermine the Everliving's confidence. It explained Koll's sudden furious attack. He felt she had to be silenced then and there to preserve the goals of the Voice of Action. Oganoon trackers had found his body an hour later.

Nile gathered that the ranks of the Everliving had been in turmoil since. The loss of the sea patrol did nothing to calm them. They didn't suspect she had nonhuman assistants, so it appeared to them that the patrol had encountered the Tuvela on her way over from the other forest and that she'd wiped it out single-handedly before it could get out an alarm. Then a short while ago they'd begun getting reports that a small fast surface vessel was maneuvering elusively about the Drift—the Sotira sleds had kept their promise to provide her with a message courier. The Everliving naturally associated the presence of the ship with that of the Tuvela. But they didn't know what its purpose was. . . .

They'd been under psychological pressure since she'd first avoided what had seemed inevitable capture. With each move she'd made thereafter the pressure increased. That the moves were forced on her they didn't realize. All of it would seem part of the Tuvela's developing plan . . . a plan they didn't understand and seemed unable to check. They didn't know to what it would lead. Fears they'd nourished and fought down for over half a century fed heavily on them again.

So they, the proud Palachs of Porad Anz, had sent out Dr. Ticos Cay and a delegation of the Voice of Caution to offer the Tuvela a cessation of hostilities and the opportunity to present the Guardians' terms to them in person. No doubt some of Koll's adherents remained ragingly opposed to the move.

Could she risk talking to them?

As things stood, she had a very good chance of getting away from here presently. Then she could warn her kind that there was an enemy among them and that they must prepare for attack. If she walked into the enemy's camp and couldn't maintain the Tuvela bluff, she'd have thrown away the chance. If Ticos had understood that, he mightn't be urging her now to reveal herself.

But if she didn't respond and remained concealed, the pressure on the Everliving wouldn't let down. They'd interpret silence to mean that they were no longer being offered an opportunity to withdraw. How would they react? They might feel it was too late to attempt retreat. They'd had many weeks to prepare the strike against Nandy-Cline from their hidden floatwood bases. If they decided to launch it before countermoves began, how long would it be before space weapons lashed out at the mainland? Hours? Her warning would come too late in that case.

The real question might be whether she could risk *not* talking to them.

Abruptly, Nile made up her mind.

The Parahuan boat came slowly around the curve of the forest. The loudspeaker began to shout again. After a few words it stopped. The Palach Moga, standing beside Ticos Cay, lowered the instrument carefully and turned it off with an air of preferring to make no sudden moves. There was a burst of sibilant whisperings behind Ticos. They ceased. The boat's engines cut out and it drifted up against a tangle of lagoon weeds. The man and the six aliens stared at the motionless figure standing at the forest's edge ten yards away.

The Tuvela's voice said crisply, "Dr. Cay!"

Ticos cleared his throat. "Yes, Guardian?"

"Have that craft brought over here and introduce the Parahuan officers to me—"

Stepping down into the boat was like crossing the threshold of a grotesque dream. They stood erect on long legs, abandoning the natural posture of their kind, balanced not too certainly on broad feet. Parahuan heads inclined in obeisance to the Guardian as Ticos introduced them in turn. She knew the names of the Palach Moga and one of the others from his report. Along with half a dozen Great Palachs, Moga was the most influential member of the Voice of Caution. He retained his place beside Ticos. The others stood well to the back of the boat as it turned out again into the lagoon.

Moga spoke briefly into a communicator, said to Nile, "The Everliving are assembling to hear the Guardian. . . ."

She didn't ask where they were assembling. A Tuvela would show no concern for such details. An angry whistling came for an instant from farther out in the lagoon. Sweeting still didn't approve of this move.

The sound seemed to jar all along Nile's nerves. She was frightened; and knowing that now of all times she couldn't afford to be frightened simply was making it that much worse. For moments her thoughts became a shifting blur of anxieties. She tried to force them back to what she would say to the Everliving, to anticipate questions to which she must have answers. It didn't work too well. But the physical reactions faded gradually again.

Stocky Oganoon figures, weapons formally displayed, lined the sides of the water-level entrance to the block-house. The boat moved a few yards along a tunnel, was moored to a platform. She followed Moga up into the structure. Ticos stayed a dozen steps behind, effacing himself, playing his own role. After the introductions, she hadn't spoken to him. On the next level, she realized he was no longer following.

The Palach Moga paused before a closed door.

"If the Guardian will graciously wait here . . . I will see that the Assembly is prepared. . . ."

Nile waited. After moments the door reopened and the Palach emerged. He carried something like a jeweled handbag slung by a long strap over one shoulder. Nile had the impression he was ill at ease.

"If the Guardian permits . . . There are Great Palachs beyond this door. They are unarmed. They would prefer it if the Guardian did not address them with a weapon at her hand."

If she couldn't convince them, Nile thought, she would die behind that door. But a Tuvela would not need to draw courage from a gun at this stage—and the UW by itself was not going to get her back past the clusters of guards in the passages behind them. She unclipped the holster from her belt, held it out. Moga placed it carefully in the bag and drew open the door. Nile went inside.

For a moment she had the impression of being in the anteroom to a great, dimly lit hall—too large a hall by far to be part of this structure in the floatwood. Then she knew that the whole opposite wall of the room was a viewscreen. There were upward of a dozen Great Palachs in the room with her, squatting along the wall to either side . . . creatures not much larger than Koll, in richly colored stiff robes and an assortment of equally colorful hats. The remainder of the Everliving, Palachs and Great Palachs of all degrees, were arranged in rows along the hall, which must be a section of the headquarters ship below the sea. Shallow water shifted and gleamed here and there among the rows. Motionless and silent, the massed amphibians stared up at her from the dimness.

Nile heard the door through which she had come close

quietly at her back. And curiously, with the tiny click her uncertainties were gone. A cool light clarity seemed to settle on her mind, every thought and emotion falling into place. . . . She discovered she had moved forward and was standing in the center of the chamber, facing the big screen.

Selecting her words with chilled precision, the Tuvela began to speak.

7

THE OUTSTANDING feature of the big room in the blockhouse structure the Parahuans had assigned Ticos Cay as his working laboratory was its collection of living specimens. The floatwood island's life forms lined three of the walls and filled long shelf stands in between. Neatly labeled and charted, they perched on or clung to their original chunks of floatwood, stood rooted in the pockets of forest mold or in victimized life forms in which they had been found, floated in lagoon water, clustered under transparent domes. They varied from the microscopic to inhis organisms with a thirty foot spread. For the most part, they were in biological stasis—metabolism retarded by a factor of several million, balance maintained by enzyme control and a variety of other checks. Proper handling would otherwise have been impossible.

The Guardian was able to find little fault with the progress Dr. Cay had made in his work projects. "In this respect you have not done badly," she acknowledged, for the benefit of whatever ears might be listening. She tapped the charts he'd offered for her inspection and dropped them into the file he'd taken them from. "It's disappointing, however, that it became necessary at last for me to intervene directly in a matter we had expected you to handle without our assistance."

"Given more time, I might have done it!" Ticos remonstrated humbly. "I was opposed by a number of intractable beings, as you know."

"I do know—having encountered one of those beings. But it was hardly a question of time. The issues were clear. If they had been presented with clarity, a rational majority of our uninvited guests would have drawn the correct conclusions and acted on them. We must count this a failure. You needn't let it concern you unduly. The excellent thoroughness of your work on the basic assignment, under somewhat limiting conditions, will offset the failure, at least in part."

Ticos mumbled his gratitude, went back with evident relief to additional explanations about his project. Nile checked her watch.

Forty-two minutes since she'd been escorted with careful courtesy from the assembly chamber to the lab and left there with Ticos. No word from the Everliving since then, and the Palach Moga hadn't shown up with her gun. Good sign or bad? While she was talking to them, she'd almost *been* a Tuvela. She'd blasted them! She'd felt exalted. There'd been no questions. The Great Palachs closest to her in the chamber had edged farther back to the walls before she was done, stirred nervously again whenever she shifted a glance in their direction.

Afterward, brief sharp letdown. No Tuvela, no Guardian. Simply a scared human in a potentially very bad spot, with much too much at stake. If she'd fumbled this in any way, made the slightest slip—

Now she was somewhere between those states, back to normal, worried enough but again busily balancing possibilities, planning as much as could be planned here.

One of the factors she'd been considering was this room

itself. It was long, wide, high, located somewhere near the top of the overall structure—she'd come up another level after leaving the chamber. It had a door at either end, probably locked now. The last could make no real difference since there was bound to be a gaggle of armed Oganoon outside each door to make sure the Guardian and her scientist didn't walk out on the conference. From the door at the left a raised walkway led to a platform some four feet above the floor near the center of the room. The Palachs, Ticos had explained, customarily stood there when they'd come to have dealings with him. Lighting came from conductor rods in ceiling and walls, primitive but efficient. Ventilation arrangements, while equally simple, met the lab's requirements perfectly. There was a large shadowy rectangle enclosed in a grid up on one of the walls just below the ceiling. Behind the grid was an unseen window, a rectangular opening in the wall. The salty-moist many-scented freshness of the floatwood forest swirled constantly about them. Enclosed without it, many of Ticos' research specimens would have died in days. But the storm gusts which occasionally set the blockhouse structure quivering were damped out at the window, and almost no sound came through.

So the shadowy rectangle was a force screen. It would let out no light, and certainly it was impenetrable to solid objects such as a human body. The screen controls must be outside the room, or Ticos would have indicated them to her. But there was a knobby protrusion on either side of the grid which enclosed the rectangle. And beneath those protrusions were the screen generators. . . .

Which brought up the matter of tools, and weapons or items which could serve as weapons. Her UW would be hard to replace in either capacity. But one could make do. Ticos had left a small cutter-sealer on the central worktable back of them. A useful all-around gadget, and one that could turn into a factor here. Another potential factor was the instrument studded with closely packed rows of tiny push-buttons, which Ticos carried attached to his belt and through which he regulated various internal balances and individual environmental requirements of his specimens.

The only obvious weapons around were the guns in the hands of three Parahuan guards who squatted stolidly in two feet of water in the partitioned end of the room at the right. From the platform, Nile had looked in briefly across the dividing wall at them. Two were faced toward the wall; one was faced away toward a long table near the second exit. None of them moved while she studied them. But they looked ready to act instantly. The guns appeared to be heavy-duty short-range blasters, made to be used by hands four times larger than hers. On the table stood Ticos Cay's communicator.

The guns weren't factors, except as they could become negative ones. But with a Sotira racing sled moving within close-contact band reach, the communicator was a very large factor. The Everliving in their nervous ambivalence had decreed it should be available at a moment's notice in case they were forced to open emergency negotiations with the Tuvelas through Dr. Cay. The guards were there to blast death into anybody who attempted to use it under any other circumstances.

Ticos Cay himself was, of course, an important factor. Physically he could become a heavy liability if matters didn't develop well. He'd lost his wiry bounciness; he was a damaged old man. His face looked drawn tight even when he smiled. He'd been holding pain out of his awareness for weeks; but as an organism he'd been afflicted with almost intolerable strains and had begun to drift down towards death. Of course he knew it.

Mentally he didn't seem much impaired. His verbal responses might be a trifle slowed but not significantly. Nile thought she still could depend on him for quick and accurate reaction, as she might have to do. Because the final factor in the calculation here was Ticos Cay's collection of floatwood life. On the worktable, next to the cutter-sealer she'd mentally earmarked, lay several objects like hardshelled wrinkled gray fruits, twice the size of her fist. Ticos had taken them out of a container to explain the purpose they were to serve in his research, left them lying there.

They were called wriggler apples and the shells showed they had ripened. The thing to know about ripe wriggler apples was that they remained quiescent until they received the specific environmental stimulus of contact with salt water. At that moment they split open. And the wrigglers came out. . . .

At best, the apples were a dubious research item. And they were not at all the only specimens in that category here. At a rough estimate, one in fifty of the life forms which cluttered the shelf stands and walls had caused Nile to flinch inwardly at first glimpse or whiff of identifying odor. Floatwood stuff she'd been conditioned against almost since she was big enough to walk. It wasn't all small or unobtrusive. Dominating the center of the room was a great purpleleafed inhis, the pale blue petals of its pseudoflowers tightly furled. A rarity, to no one's regret. In the forests, Nile wouldn't have come willingly within thirty feet of one. By classification it was a plant form. A vegetable, with lightning reactions. The sledmen, with good reason, had named it the Harpooneer. For some weeks it had loomed above and just behind the Palachs who had come and squatted on the platform, staring down at the human prisoner. . . .

It was dormant now, as were most of the other unreliable specimens—totally innocuous, metabolism slowed to a timeless pulse. In biological stasis. It would remain innocuous until it was given the precise measured stimulus, massive enzyme jolt or whatever, that broke the stasis.

And who could produce such stimuli? Why, to be sure, Dr. Cay with his push-button control device. He'd made certain that when it came time to die, he should have the means of taking some of the enemy with him.

Which might not be a detached scientific attitude but was certainly a very human one. . . .

Nile flicked another glance at her watch. Forty-three and a half minutes.

The door at the left clanged open.

The Palach Moga came first along the walkway. The bag into which the UW had disappeared swayed at his side, its strap slung over his shoulder. That detail might have been reassuring if the group behind him had looked less like an execution squad.

Nile stood with her back to the worktable, feeling tensions surge up and trying to show nothing. Ticos gave her an uncertain, questioning look, then turned and moved off slowly along the table, stopping a dozen feet away to watch the Parahuans. The fingers of his right hand fiddled absently with the control device. Moga was approaching the central platform in his grotesquely dainty upright walk, webbed feet placed carefully for each step. Two Oganoon guards came behind him, staring at Nile, massive short-barreled guns held ready for action. Two unfamiliar Palachs followed, moving in an uncompromising Parahuan waddle. Their strap harnesses were an identical crimson; and each carried two sizable handweapons, one on either side, grips turned forward. Another pair of guards concluded the procession. These had their guns slung across their backs and held items like folded black nets. A fifth guard had stopped inside the door, which had closed again after the party passed through. He had another kind of gun with a long narrow barrel, attached to a chunky tripod. He set the tripod down with a thump on the walkway, squatted behind it. The gun muzzle swung around and pointed at Nile.

She didn't move. She'd give them some reason not to trust her.

The group reached the platform, spread out. Moga stood near the platform's edge. The red-harnessed Palachs flanked him, hands clamped on their gun grips. The guards with the guns took up positions to either side of the Palachs. The guards with the black nets remained a little to the rear, at the left side of the platform. There were, Nile thought, indications of as much nervous tenseness as she was able to make out in a Parahuan visage—silently writhing speech slits, blinking atmosphere eyes. And all eyes were fixed on her, on the Tuvela. Nobody looked at Ticos Cay.

"Guardian, I shall speak first for myself," Moga's voice said suddenly.

Nile didn't answer. The voice resumed. "I am in great fear for Porad Anz. . . . When you agreed to address the Everliving, I was certain that your mission would succeed and that the Balance would shift to reason. And the response of the Assembly was strongly favorable. Your logic was persuasive. But there has been an unforeseen development. By violence the Voice of Action has assumed control of our forces. It is against all custom, an unprecedented Violation of Rules—but that appears to be no longer important. Here, on the Command Ship and elsewhere on this world, many Great Palachs and Palachs lie dead. Those who survive have submitted to the Voice of Action which now alone speaks for the Everliving. I have come to inform you of what has been decreed. And having spoken for myself, I shall speak now with the words of the Voice of Action."

Silence.

The group on the platform remained tautly motionless. Nile watched them; they stared at her. So the red-harnessed Palachs represented the Voice of Action. . . . The thought came suddenly that these must be very courageous creatures. They'd entered the laboratory to confront a legend. They were braving gromgorru. They waited now to see what the Tuvela might do in response to Moga's statement.

The Tuvela also stayed silent and motionless.

The Palach to Moga's right began speaking abruptly in a series of fluctuating Parahuan hootings, eyes fixed on Nile. After perhaps half a minute he stopped. Moga promptly began to translate.

"Whatever you call yourself, you are a Tuvela. We know this now. You have threatened Porad Anz in the name of your kind. That cannot be tolerated. You have told us that in any hostile encounter with the Guardians the Everliving must be defeated. Once and for all, that lie shall now be disproved. . . ."

Moga's voice ended. The red-harnessed Palach spoke

again. His fellow turned his head for an instant, addressed the two Oganoon holding the nets. The two took the nets from their arms, shook them out. Black straps dangled from their rims. . . .

Moga took up the translation.

"The Voice of Action offers you and Dr. Cay the death of Palachs. It is painful but honorable. If you accept, you will submit to being enclosed by the confinement nets. If you attempt to resist, you will be shot down and die here like Hulons. In either case, Tuvela, your defeat and death signal the beginning of the hour of our attack on your world. And now, if it is within the power of a Tuvela to defy our purpose, show what you can do."

Beyond the group, the Parahuan at the door sagged silently forward over the gun, head and upper body obscured by the curling green fog lifting from a specimen on the wall beside him. The armed guards on the platform had pointed their guns at Nile. The red-harnessed Palachs drew their weapons. A dozen or so of the Harpooneer's pseudoflowers behind the platform quivered and unfurled in a flick of motion like great yellow-blue eyes blinking open. Nile dropped flat.

There had been at least two guns aimed directly at her in that instant; and fast as the Harpooneer was, it might not be fast enough to keep the guns from going off.

They didn't go off. There were other sounds instead. Something landed with a thump on the floor not far away. With a brief shock of surprise her mind recorded the bag Moga had been carrying. She was coming back up on her feet by then, scooped two of the gray-shelled wriggler apples from the worktable, lobbed them across the partitioning wall into the flooded section of the room. She heard them splash. A detached part of her awareness began counting off seconds. She looked around.

They were dead up there, nervous systems frozen, unlidded double-lensed eyes staring hugely. Embedded in their backs were bone-white spikes, tipping the thick coiled tendrils extended from the pseudoflowers. Four still stood swaying, transfixed, long legs stretched out rigidly. Three had been lifted from the platform, were being drawn over to the Harpooneer. Nile upended Moga's bag, shook out the UW, had it clipped to her climb-belt as the part of her mind that was counting seconds reached thirty and stopped. There'd been a few violent splashings from beyond the partition, but she heard nothing now. Ticos, holding the control device in both hands, face taut and white, gave her a quick nod.

The climb-belt was at half-weight as she reached the partition wall. She jumped, clapped her hands to the top, went up and over.

Seven years before, she'd seen a wriggler swarm hit a human diver. It was largely a matter of how close one happened to be to the apple when it tumbled down out of the floatwood forest, struck salt water and split. In the same moment thousands of tiny writhing black lines spilled from it and flashed unerringly toward any sizable animal bodies in the immediate vicinity, striking like a cluster of needle drills, puncturing thick hide or horny scales in instants.

The three guards lay face down, partly submerged, in the water that covered the floor. Two were motionless. The third quivered steadily, something like a haze of black fur still extending along his torso below the surface. All three were paralyzed now, would be dead in minutes as the swarms spread through them, feeding as they went.

And the passage was safe for Nile. The wrigglers were committed.

She reached the stand with Ticos' communicator on it, flipped switches, turned dials, paused an instant to steady her breath.

"Sotira-Doncar!" she said into the speaker then. "Sotira-Doncar! *Parahuans here! Parahuans here!*" And cut off the communicator.

No time to wait for a reply. No time at all—

"Can you needle the stink-fogs into action?"

"Of course. But—"

"Hit them!" Nile drew the climb-belt tight around his waist, clipped the UW to the top of her trunks. "If we can get out, we'll be out before it hurts us."

Ticos glanced up at the force-screened window oblong, grunted dubiously. "Hope you're right!" His finger tapped a control. "They're hit. Now?"

Nile bent, placed her hands together. "Foot up! Try to keep your balance. You're minim-weight—you'll go up fast. Latch on to the grid and drop me the belt. I think I can make it to your ankles."

She put all her strength into the heave. He did go up fast, caught the grid and hooked an arm through it. The climb-belt floated back down. Greasy clouds boiled about the aroused stink-fogs near the entrance door on the left as Nile snatched the belt out of the air and fastened it around herself. Ticos was hanging by both hands now, legs stretched down. She sprang, sailed up along the wall, gripped his ankles and swarmed up him, the antigrav field again enclosing both of them. Moments later she'd worked her knees over a grid bar, had the belt back around Ticos.

Breathing hard, he pulled himself up beside her and reached for the control device.

"Fogging up down there, all right!" he wheezed. "Can't see the door. Might alert a few more monsters, eh?"

"Any you can without killing us." Somebody outside the room *must* know by now that the execution plans had hit a snag. Clinging by knees and left hand, Nile placed the UW's muzzle against one of the grid casings that should have a force screen generator beneath it, held the trigger down. The beam hissed and spat. The casing glowed, turned white. An incredible blending of stenches rose about her suddenly, closing her throat, bringing water to her eyes. She heard Ticos splutter and cough.

Then the casing gave. Something inside shattered and flared. Wind roared in above Nile, salty and fresh.

"Up and out, Ticos! Screen's gone!" She hauled herself up, flung an arm across the ledge. Her shoulder tingled abruptly. Nerve charge! Parahuans in the lab. . . . Below her, Ticos made a sound of distress. Straddling the ledge, she squinted down, saw him blurrily. He'd dropped the control gadget, was clinging to the grid with both hands, shaking in hard convulsions. Heart hammering, Nile reached for him, caught his arm, brought the low-weight body flopping over the ledge and into the growth outside the window. He grasped some branches, was steadying himself, as she turned back.

Half the lab below was obscured by stink-fog emissions, whirled about by the wind. There was an outburst of desperate hootings—one or more Parahuans had run into a specimen which wasn't bothered by smells. She had glimpses of bulky shapes milling about, blinded by the fog. They should also be half-strangled by it. But at least one of them had seen Ticos up here long enough to take aim with a nerve gun. . . .

The greasy mist swirled aside from a section of floor where four glassy containers stood on a low table. Nile had seen what was inside them when she came into the lab. The top of the nearest container splintered instantly now under the UW's beam. She shifted aim. The startled organism in the shattered container already was contracting and expanding energetically like a pump. A second container cracked. As Nile sighted on a third one, a Parahuan reeled out of the stink-fog cloud, swung a big gun up at the window.

She ducked back behind the ledge. No time for gun duels. And no need. Two of the containers were broken and she'd seen jets of pale vapor spurting from both. The specimens in them were called acid bombs, with good reason. Nobody in the lab at present was likely to leave it alive—and certainly no one coming in for a while was going to get out again in good enough condition to report that the captives had fled by way of the force screen window.

She aimed along the room's ceiling to a point where the central lighting bars intersected. Something exploded there, and the lab was plunged into darkness.

Nile swung back from the window, the stink-fog's reek wafting about her. Ticos was leaning against branches, clinging to them, making abrupt jerking motions.

"How badly are you hit?" she asked quickly.

He grunted. "I don't know! I'm no weapons specialist. What *did* hit me? Something like a neural agitator?"

"In that class. You didn't stop a full charge, or you wouldn't be on your feet. With the climb-belt, I can carry you. But if you can move—"

"I can move. I seem able to hold off some of the effects. If I don't slow you down too much."

"Let's try it out," Nile said. "They shouldn't be after us immediately. Let me know if it gets too difficult. . . ."

Her bundle was in the niche of floatwood where she'd left it. She opened it hastily. Ticos stood behind her, clinging to the vegetation, bent over and gasping for breath. Nile was winded enough herself. They'd scrambled straight up from the roof of the blockhouse into the forest, cut across south of the sea-haval rookery, clambered down again toward the lagoon. It hadn't been a lightweight dance along the branches for her this time. Her muscles knew they'd been working. Even so, Ticos, supported by the climb-belt, had been pushed very hard to keep up with her. He wasn't equipped with dark-lenses, wasn't sufficiently skilled in the use of the belt; and at intervals the nerve gun charge he'd absorbed set off spasms of uncontrollable jerking and shaking. There were antidotes for the last, and no doubt the Parahuans had them. But there was nothing available here. He'd have to work it out. Another five or ten minutes of climbing might do it, Nile thought. It had better do it: she knew now Ticos had lost half his reserves of physical energy since she'd seen him last. If the effects of the alien weapon corresponded at all closely to those of its humanly produced counterparts, a more central charge should have killed him quickly. The load he'd stopped might still do it, though that seemed much less likely now.

She fished the pack of dark-lens gel from the pouch, handed it to him. "Better put on your night eyes."

"Huh? Oh! Thanks. I can use those."

A series of shrill whistles rose from the lagoon. Ticos' head turned quickly.

"Sounded almost like one of your otters!"

"It was. Sweeting." Nile had heard intermittent whistling for the past several minutes, hadn't mentioned it. The wind still drowned out most other sounds. She pried the end of the buti stem open with her knife. "Got the lenses in place?"

"Yes."

"Then let's see how fast you can put on a coat of buti. We might have a problem here rather soon."

Ticos took the stem, began rubbing sap hurriedly over his clothes. "Parahuans?" he asked.

"Perhaps. Something seems to be coming this way along the lagoon. That was Sweeting's warning signal. Did you know your friends had a tarm here?"

"I've seen it." Ticos' tone held shock, but he didn't stop working. "You think that's what's—"

"It's more likely to be the tarm than Parahuans."

"What can we do, Nile?"

"Buti seems to be good cover if it doesn't see us. The thing got close to me once before. If it comes this far, it probably will find our trail. I'll go see what Sweeting has to tell. You finish up with the buti. But don't smear the stuff on your shoe soles yet."

"Why not?"

"I think we can lose the tarm here. It may not be too healthy by now anyway."

He looked up briefly, made a sound that was almost a laugh.

"More Tuvela work?"

"This Tuvela has little helpers. . . ." Nile switched on the otter-caller, moved quickly toward the lagoon. At the edge of the water she stood glancing about, listening. Nothing significant to be seen. The blurred snarling of engines

123

came for a moment from the general direction of the block-house. Then Sweeting broke the surface below her.

"Nile, you watch out! Tarm's coming!"

Nile rejoined Ticos moments later. The tarm was approaching through the floatwood above water level. It might be casting about for their trail, or might be on the move simply because it was beginning to feel the effects of the wild otters' weed poison. They'd succeeded in planting a considerable number of the thorns in it under the block-house. Sweeting reported its motions seemed sluggish. But for a while it could still be dangerous enough.

She postponed further explanations, and Ticos didn't press for any. They hurried down to the lagoon together. If the tarm didn't turn aside, it should come across their human trail. Then the lagoon must be where the trail seemed to end. If it began searching for them in the water, the otters would try to finish it off. Evidently the tarm didn't realize that the small elusive creatures might be dangerous to it. After it found it couldn't catch them, it hadn't paid them much attention.

They rubbed buti sap into the soles of their shoes, waves lapping a few feet below. Nile thought the last coating she'd given herself should be adequate otherwise. Her stock of the sap was running out; she might need some later and didn't know whether she could find another stand. By the time they finished, otter whistling had begun again, not far off. She led the way back into the forest, moving upward. Ticos crowded behind her, tarm fear overriding his fatigue. Perhaps a hundred feet on, Nile suddenly checked.

"Down, Ticos! Flatten out!"

She dropped beside him on the bough along which they

had been moving. There was a disturbance in the forest below that wasn't caused by the wind. Vegetation thrashed heavily. The noise stopped for some seconds, then resumed. It seemed to be approaching the area they'd left. They watched, heads raised, motionless.

Then Nile saw the tarm for the third time. Ticos stiffened beside her. He'd detected it too.

Even with the dark-lenses she couldn't make out many details. There was growth between them. The great thing moving among the boles of the forest looked like a fat gliding worm. Its nearness had an almost numbing effect on her again. She stared at it in fixed fascination; and it was some moments then before she realized it had stopped—about at the point where they had gone down to the water, where the human scent lay and where it should end, blotted out by the buti.

They both started at an abrupt series of loud sucking noises. The pale mass seemed to swell, then flattened. It had turned, was flowing up into the forest. Ticos swallowed audibly.

"It's—"

"Going back the way we came. It isn't following us."

He sighed with relief. They watched the tarm move out of sight. Long seconds passed. Finally Ticos looked over at Nile. She shook her head. Better not stir just yet. . . .

And then the tarm reappeared, following the line of their trail back to the water's edge. Now it slid unhesitatingly down into the lagoon and sank below the surface. Otter whistles gave it greeting.

They got to their feet at once, hurried on. The wind noises had become allies, covering the sounds of their retreat. Nile selected the easiest routes—broad boughs, slanted trunks. Ticos simply wasn't up to much more; he stumbled, slipped, breathed in wheezing gasps. At last she stopped to let him rest.

"Huh?" he asked. "What's the delay?"

"We don't have to kill you at this stage," Nile told him. "They may not even know yet that we aren't lying dead in the laboratory. They've probably sealed the doors to keep half their fort from becoming contaminated."

He grunted. "If they haven't searched the lab yet, they soon will! They can get protective equipment there in a hurry. And someone should have thought of that window by now."

Nile shrugged. The tarm could chill her, but she was no longer too concerned about Parahuan trackers. "We have a good head start," she said. "If they trail us to the lagoon, they won't know where to look next. We could be any-where on the island." She hesitated. "If they have any sense left, they won't waste any more time with us at all. They'll just get their strike against the mainland rolling. That's what I'm afraid they'll do."

Ticos made a giggling sound. "That's the one thing they can't do now! Not for a while."

"Why not?"

"It's the way their minds work. The only justification the Voice of Action had for what it's done was the fact that it could deliver your head. Proof of the argument—Tuvelas can be destroyed! They've lost the proof and they'll be de-bating for hours again before they're up to making another move. Except, of course, to look for you. They'll be doing that, and doing it intensively. We'd better not wait around.

They might get lucky. How far is it still to the incubator?"

Nile calculated. "Not much more than four hundred yards. But it includes some pretty stiff scrambling."

"Let's scramble," Ticos said. "I'll last that far."

8

THE INCUBATOR was a loosely organized colony-animal which looked like a globular deformity of the floatwood bough about which it grew. The outer surface of the globe was a spiky hedge. Inside was a rounded hollow thirty feet in diameter, containing seed pods and other vital parts, sketchily interconnected. The hedge's spikes varied from finger-long spines to three foot daggers, mounted on individually mobile branches. Only two creatures big and powerful enough to be a potential threat to the incubator's internal sections were known to have found a way of penetrating the hedge. One of them was man.

The other was no enemy. It was a flying kester, a bony animal with a sixteen foot wingspread, at home among the ice floes of the south, which maintained a mutually beneficial relationship with the incubator organism. Periodically it flew northward to meet floatwood islands coming along the Meral, sought out the incubators installed on them, left one of its leathery eggs in a seed pod on each, finally returned to its cold skies. In the process it had distributed the incubators' fertilizing pollen among the colonies, thereby carrying out its part of the instinctual bargain. When the young kester hatched, the seed pod produced a sap to nourish the future pollinator until it left its foster parent and took to the air.

Man's energy weapons could get him undamaged through

the hedge. The simpler way was to pretend to be a polar kester.

"It's right behind these bushes," Nile said. She indicated a section of the guard hedge curving away above the shrubbery before them. "Don't get much closer to it."

"I don't intend to!" Ticos assured her. Their approach had set off a furious rattling as of many dry bones being beaten together. The incubator was agitating its armament in warning. Ticos stood back watching as Nile finished trimming a ten foot springy stalk she'd selected to gain them passage through the hedge. Another trick learned in childhood—the shallows settlers considered incubator seeds and polar kester eggs gourmet items. Spiky fronds at the tip of the stalk were a reasonable facsimile of the spines on the kester's bony wing-elbow. Confronted by an incubator's challenge, the kester would brush its elbow back and forth along one of the waving hedge branches. A number of such strokes identified the visitor and admitted it to the globe's interior.

Nile moved up to the shrubs standing across their path on the floatwood bough, parted them cautiously. The rattling grew louder and something slashed heavily at the far side of the shrubs. She thrust out the stalk, touched the fronds to an incubator branch, stroked it lightly. After some seconds the branch stiffened into immobility. Moments later, so did the branches immediately about it. The rattling gradually died away. Nile continued the stroking motion. Suddenly the branches opposite her folded back, leaving an opening some five feet high and three wide.

They slipped through, close together. Nile turned, tapped the interior of the hedge with the stalk. The opening closed again.

Unaided human eyes would have recorded blackness here. The dark-lenses still showed them as much as they needed to see. "Over there," Nile said, nodding.

The interior of the colony-animal was compartmentalized by sheets of oily tissue, crisscrossed by webbings of fibrous cables. In a compartment on their left were seven of the big gourd-shaped seed pods. The caps of all but two stood tilted upward, indicating they contained neither fertilized seeds nor an infant kester.

"We settle down in those?" It was Ticos' first experience inside an incubator.

"You do," Nile said. "They're clean and comfortable if you don't mind being dusted with pollen a bit. The whole incubator has built-in small-vermin repellents. We could camp here indefinitely."

"It doesn't object to being tramped around in?"

"If it's aware of being tramped around in, it presumably thinks there's a kester present. Go ahead!"

He grunted, gripped one of the cables, stepped off the bough to another cable and swayed over to the nearest pod. Nile came behind, waited while he scrambled up the pod, twisted about, let himself down inside and found footing. "Roomy enough," he acknowledged, looking over the edge at her. He wiped sweat from his face, sighed. "Here, let me give you back your belt."

"Thanks." Nile fastened the climb-belt about her. "Where's yours, by the way?"

"Hid it out in my quarters when I saw the raiding party come up. Thought I might have use for it later. But I never got an opportunity to pick it up again. It's probably still there."

"How do you feel now?"

Ticos shrugged. "I've stopped twitching. Otherwise—
physically exhausted, mentally alert. Uncomfortably alert,
as a matter of fact. I gather you've had experience with
nerve guns?"

"Our kinds," said Nile. "The Parahuan item seem to produce the same general pattern of effects."

"Including mental hyperstimulation?"

"Frequently. If it's a light charge, a grazing shot—which
is what you caught. The stimulation should shift to drowsi-
ness suddenly. When it does, don't fight it. Just settle down
in the pod, curl up and go to sleep. That's the best medicine
for you at present."

"Not at present!" Ticos said decidedly. "Now that we've
hit a lull in the action, you can start answering some questions. That ship you may have contacted—"

"A sledman racer. It was waiting for a message from me."

"Why? How did it happen to be there?"

Nile told him as concisely as possible. When she finished,
he said, "So nobody out there has really begun to suspect
what's going on. . . ."

"With the possible exception of Tuvelas," Nile said dryly.

"Yes, the Tuvelas. Gave you quite an act to handle there,
didn't I?"

"You did. But it kept me from being clobbered in the air.
The Parahuans have been creating the recent communication disturbances?"

"They've been adding to the natural ones. Part of the
Great Plan. They're familiar with the comm systems in use
here. They worked out the same general systems on their
own water worlds centuries ago. So they know how to go
about disrupting them."

"What's the purpose?"

"Testing their interference capability. Conditioning the humans to the disturbances. Just before they strike, they intend to blank out the planet. No outgoing messages. Knock off spaceships attempting to leave or coming in. Before anyone outside the system gets too concerned about the silence, they intend to be in control."

Nile looked at him, chilled. "That might work, mightn't it?"

"Up to that point it might. I'm no trained strategist, but I believe the local defenses aren't too impressive."

"They aren't designed to deal with major invasions."

"Then if the Voice of Action can maintain the previous organization—coordinate the attack, execute it in planned detail—I should think they could take Nandy-Cline. Even hold it a while. The situation might still be very much touch and go in that respect. Of course the probability is that they killed too many dissenting Palachs tonight to leave their military apparatus in good working condition. And in the long run the Great Plan is idiotic. Porad Anz and its allies don't have a reasonable chance against the Hub."

"Are you sure of that?"

"I am. Take their own calculations. They've studied us. They've obtained all the information they could, in every way they could, and they've analyzed it in exhaustive detail. So they wound up with the Tuvela Theory. A secretly maintained strain of superstrategists. . . ."

"I don't see how they ever got to the theory," Nile said. "There isn't really a shred of evidence for it."

"From the Palachs' point of view there's plenty of evidence. It was a logical conclusion when you consider that with very few exceptions they're inherently incapable of accepting the real explanation: that on the level of galactic competition their species is now inferior to ours. They've frozen their structure of civilization into what they consider a pattern of perfection. When they meet conditions with which the pattern doesn't cope, they can't change it. To attempt to change perfection would be unthinkable. They met such conditions in their first attempt to conquer Hub worlds. They failed then. They'd meet the same conditions now. So they'd fail again."

"They've acquired allies," Nile said.

"Very wobbly ones. Porad Anz could never get established well enough to draw them into the action. And they're showing sense. Various alien civilizations tried to grab off chunks of the Hub while the humans were busy battling one another during the War Centuries. All accounts indicate the intruders got horribly mangled. How do you account for it?"

Nile shrugged. "Easily enough. They got in the way of a family fight, and the family had been conditioned to instant wholesale slaughter for generations. It isn't surprising they didn't do well. But frankly I've begun to wonder how prepared we'd be generally to handle that kind of situation now. The nearest thing to a war the Hub's known for a long time is when some subgovernment decides it's big enough for autonomy and tries to take on the Federation. And they're always squelched so quickly you can hardly call it a fight."

"So they are," Ticos agreed. "What do you think of the Federation's Overgovernment?"

She hesitated. One of the least desirable aftereffects of a nerve gun charge that failed to kill could be gradually developing mental incoherence. If it wasn't given prompt attention, it could result in permanent derangement. She suspected Ticos might be now on the verge of rambling. If so, she'd better keep him talking about realities of one kind or another until he was worked safely past that point. She said, "That's a rather general question, isn't it? I'd say I simply don't think about the Overgovernment much."

"Why not?"

"Well, why should I? It doesn't bother me and it seems able to do its job—as witness those squelched rebellious subgovernments."

"It maintains the structure of the Federation," Ticos said, "because we learned finally that such a structure was absolutely necessary. Tampering with it isn't tolerated. Even the suggestion of civil war above the planetary level isn't tolerated. The Overgovernment admittedly does that kind of thing well. But otherwise you do hear a great many complaints. A recurrent one is that it doesn't do nearly enough to control the criminal elements of the population."

Nile shook her head. "I don't agree! I've worked with the Federation's anticrime agencies here. They're efficient enough. Of course they can't handle everything. But I don't think the Overgovernment could accomplish much more along those lines without developing an oppressive bureaucratic structure—which I certainly wouldn't want."

"You feel crime control should be left up to the local citizenry?"

"Of course it should, when it's a local problem. Criminals aren't basically different from other problems we have around. We can deal with them. We do it regularly."

Ticos grunted. "Now that," he remarked, "is an attitude almost no Palach would be able to understand! And it seems typical of our present civilization." He paused. "You'll recall I used to wonder why the Federation takes so little obvious interest in longevity programs, eugenics projects and the like."

She gave him a quick glance. Not rambling, after all? "You see a connection?"

"A definite one. When it comes to criminals, the Overgovernment doesn't actually encourage them. But it maintains a situation in which the private citizen is invited to handle the problems they create. The evident result is that criminality remains a constant threat but is kept within tolerable limits. Which is merely a small part of the overall picture. Our society fosters aggressive competitiveness on almost all levels of activity; and the Overgovernment rarely seems too concerned about the absolute legality of methods used in competition. The limits imposed usually are imposed by agreements among citizen organizations, which also enforce them."

"You feel all this is a kind of substitute for warfare?"

"It's really more than a substitute," Ticos said. "A society under serious war stresses tends to grow rigidly controlled and the scope of the average individual is correspondingly reduced. In the kind of balanced anarchy in which we live now, the individual's scope is almost as wide as he wants to make it or his peers will tolerate. For the large class of non-aggressive citizens who'd prefer simply to be allowed to go about their business and keep out of trouble, that's a non-optimum situation. They're presented with many unpleasant problems they don't want, are endangered and occasionally harassed or destroyed by human predators. But in the long run the problems never really seem to get out of hand. Because we also have highly aggressive antipredators. Typically, they don't prey on the harmless citizen. But their hackles go up when they meet their mirror image, the predator—from whom they can be distinguished mainly by their goals. When there are no official restraints on them, they appear to be as a class more than a match for the predators. As you say, you handle your criminals here on Nandy-Cline. Wherever the citizenry is making a real effort, they seem to be similarly handled. On the whole our civilization flourishes." He added, "There are shadings and variations to all this, of course. The harmless citizen, the predator and the antipredator are ideal concepts. But the pattern exists and is being maintained."

"So what's the point?" Nile asked. "If it's maintained deliberately, it seems rather cruel."

"It has abominably cruel aspects, as a matter of fact. However, as a species," said Ticos, "man evolved as a very tough, alert and adaptable creature, well qualified to look out for what he considered his interests. The War Centuries honed those qualities. They're being even more effectively honed today. I think it's done deliberately. The Overgovernment evidently isn't interested in establishing a paradisiac environment for the harmless citizen. Its interest is in the overall quality of the species. And man as a species remains an eminently dangerous creature. The Overgovernment restricts it no more than necessity indicates. So it doesn't support the search for immortality—immortality would change the creature. In what way, no one can really say. Eugenics should change it, so eugenics projects aren't really favored, though they aren't interfered with. I think the Overgovernment prefers the species to continue to evolve in its own way. On the record, it's done well. They don't want to risk eliminating genetic possibilities which may be required eventually to keep it from encountering some competitive species as an inferior."

Nile said after a pause, "Well, that's mainly speculation, Ticos."

"Of course it is. But it's no speculation to say that the Hub still has its Tuvelas and that they're as thoroughly conditioned to act at peak performance as they ever were in the pre-Federation days. Further, there's now a relatively huge number of them around. That's what makes the position of the Parahuans and their potential allies impossible. They aren't opposed by a narrow caste of Guardians. They'd hit automatic Tuvela strategy again wherever and whenever they tried to strike. A few, a very few, of the Palachs realized that. Moga was one of them. That's why he killed himself."

"Moga killed himself?"

"At the crucial moment in the lab," Ticos said, "you rather cravenly dropped flat on your face. Since nobody was pointing a gun at me, I remained standing and watched. Moga couldn't foresee exactly what would happen, but I knew he'd been aware of the purpose of my specimens for some time. He understood that he and the group which came into the lab with him would have to die if we were to escape. We had to escape to keep the Voice of Action checked. When the moment came, Moga was quite ready. The others didn't find time to squeeze their gun studs. He found time to pitch that bag at you so you would get your gun back. You see, he knew you were a very competent but still very vulnerable human being. He didn't believe at all in the legend of the invincible Tuvela. But he had to do what he could to help preserve the legend. He had a cold, hopeless hatred for humanity because he had realized it was the superior species. And, as he said, he was in deathly fear for Porad Anz. The Everliving as a whole were simply unable to understand that mankind could be superior to them. The concept had no meaning. But they could be persuaded to withdraw if they became convinced that the freakish supermen who ruled humanity were truly invincible. So, in effect, Moga conspired with me, and later with you, to produce that impression on them. . . ."

He paused, shook his head, yawned deeply. Nile watched him.

"You see, I . . . uh, what . . ." His voice trailed off. His eyes were half closed now, lids flickering. After a moment his head began to sag.

"How do you feel?" she asked.

"Huh?" Ticos raised his head again, shook it. "I don't know," he said hesitantly. "There was—mental confusion for a moment . . . swirling bright lights. Don't quite know how to describe it." He drew a deep breath. "Part of the nerve charge effect, I suppose?"

"Yes, it is," she said. "Neural agitators are dirty weapons. You never know what the results will be. The particular kind of thing you're experiencing can build up for hours. When it does, it may cause permanent brain damage."

Ticos shrugged irritably. "What can I do about it? I've been blocking the stuff, but it seems to be leaking through to me now."

"Sleep's indicated. Plenty of sleep—preferably not less than a day or two. After that you should be all right again."

"The problem there," Ticos said, "is that I don't believe I'll be able to sleep without drugs. And we don't—" He glanced at her. "Or do we?"

"We do. I saw balath seeds on the way here and brought a few along."

He grunted. "Think of everything, don't you? Well, I'll

be no good to the cause in the shape I'm in; that's obvious. Better give me the balath and get on about your Tuvela business. Try to make it back here though, will you?"

"I will." The natural end to the balath sleep was death. For the human organism, in about a week. Ticos knew that if she couldn't get him to the mainland and to antidotes presently, he wouldn't wake up again.

He took three soft-shelled seeds from her hand, said, "Hold your breath—good luck!" and cracked them between his fingers, close to his face. Nile heard him breathe deeply as the balath fumes drifted out from the seeds. Then he sighed, slumped back and slid down out of sight into the pod. After a few seconds, the pod cover closed over the vacated opening. . . . Well, he'd be as safe in there for a while as he could be anywhere in this area.

She reset the belt, checked her gear. Then paused a moment, head turned up. Something—a brief muffled thudding, as much body sensation as sound. It seemed to come from the sky. She'd heard similar sounds twice before while Ticos was talking. Evidently he hadn't heard them. They might have been the rumble of thunder, but she didn't think it was thunder.

Lightweight again, she moved back quickly along the living cables to the floatwood bough which intersected the incubator and on to the barrier hedge. She laid her hands for a moment against the hedge's branches. They opened quietly for her, and she slipped out into the forest.

For a minute she stood glancing about and listening. The thudding noise hadn't been repeated and there were no other indications of abnormal activity about. A great racket was starting up in the sea-haval rookery; but the sea-havals, young and old, needed no abnormal activities to set them off. Nile descended quickly through the forest until she heard water surge and gurgle below, then moved back to the lagoon.

The sky was almost cloudless now, blazing with massed starshine. She gazed about the lagoon from cover. At the base of the forest across from her a string of tiny bright-blue lights bobbed gently up and down. Were they looking for her over there? She twisted the otter caller.

Sweeting appeared, bubbling and hunting-happy, eager to be given fresh instructions. The tarm was dying or dead. The otters had rammed a fresh battery of poison thorns into it when it came out into the water, and shortly afterward it sank to the lagoon's root floor, turned on its side and stopped moving. Next they discovered a large group of armed Parahuans prowling about the floating pads and other vegetation in the central area of the lagoon. The otters accompanied them in the water, waiting for opportunities to strike. Opportunities soon came. By the time the search party grew aware of losses in its ranks, eight lifeless Oganoon had been left wedged deep among the root tangles. . . .

"You didn't let yourselves be seen?"

Sweeting snorted derisively.

"Waddle-foot jumps into water. Doesn't come up. Is sad, heh? Sea-haval eat him? Guardian Etland eat him? No otters there then."

Nile could picture it. A subsurface swirl in the dark water, three or four slashes, another flopping body hauled quickly down toward the roots . . . and no slightest indication of the nature of the attacker. The remaining Parahuans had bunched up together on the pads, keeping well away from the water. When lights began to flash and several boats approached, bristling with guns, Sweeting and her companions moved off. From a distance they watched the boats take the search party away.

Presently then: "Bloomp-bloomp! Big gun—"

Which explained the thudding noises Nile had heard. Great geysers boiled up suddenly from the area where the Parahuans had been waylaid. The fire came from a hidden emplacement on the far side of the lagoon. Sweeting described pale flares of light, soft heavy thumps of discharge. A medium energy gun—brought into action in hopes of destroying what? The Tuvela? The Palachs would have no other explanation for what had happened out there. And if they'd realized by now that their great tarm was also among the dead or missing . . .

"What were they shooting at later?" she asked.

Sweeting tilted her nose at the sky, gave the approximate otter equivalent of a shrug. "Up there! Kesters. . . ."

"Kesters?"

Kesters it seemed to have been. Perhaps the gun crew had picked up a high-flying migratory flock in its instruments and mistaken it for human vehicles. In any case, some time after the discharge a rain of charred and dismembered kester bodies briefly sprinkled the lagoon surface.

Nile chewed her lip. Parrol couldn't possibly be about the area yet, and that some other aircar should have chanced to pass by at this particular time was simply too unlikely. It looked like a case of generally jittery nerves and growing demoralization. Ticos had questioned whether the Voice of Action would be able to maintain the organization of the forces which were now under its sole control.

"And this last time?" she asked. Water stirred at her left as she spoke. She glanced over, saw that the wild otter pair had joined them, lifted a hand in greeting. They grinned silently, drifted closer.

"Wasn't us," Sweeting told her. The fire had been directed into the lagoon again, near the western end of the island. The otters hadn't been anywhere near those waters. Another panic reaction?

"What are they doing over there?" Nile asked. She nodded to the north, across the lagoon. The pinpricks of blue light had continued to move slowly along the base of the forest.

The otters had investigated them. A flotilla of small submersibles had appeared, presumably dispatched by the great command ship in the depths. Each was marked by one of the lights—purpose unknown. They were stationing sentries in pairs along the edge of the forest.

Nile considered it. The beginning of a major organized drive to encircle the Tuvela in the lagoon, assuming the energy gun hadn't got rid of her? It seemed improbable. Sentries normally were put out for defensive purposes. They had at least one gun emplacement over there, perhaps other posts that looked vulnerable to them. They might be wondering whether the Tuvela would presently come out of the water and start doing something about those posts. . . .

How open were the sentries to attack?

The otters had been considering the point when Sweeting picked up Nile's signal. The Parahuans were stationed above water level, at varying heights. One pair squatted on a floatwood stub not much more than fifteen feet above the lift of the waves. There was no visual contact between most of the posts.

Nile had seen Spiff and Sweeting drive up twenty-five feet from the surface of the sea to pluck skimming kesters out of the air. . . .

"If you can pick off that one pair before they squawk," she said, "do it. It will keep the rest of them interested in that side of the lagoon for a while. Stay away from there afterward . . . and don't bother any other waddle-feet until you hear from me."

They agreed. "What you doing now, Nile?" Sweeting asked.

"Getting a fire started so Dan can find us."

9

SHE MOVED steadily upward. The ancient floatwood trunks swayed and creaked in the wind; lesser growth rustled and whispered. The uneasy lapping of the ocean receded gradually below.

When she had come high enough, she turned toward the sea-haval rookery. The thickest sections of the oilwood stand rose somewhat beyond it. A swirl of the wind brought the rookery's stenches simmering about her. Vague rumblings rose through the forest. The area was quieter than it had been in early evening, but the gigantic feedings and the periodic uproar connected with them would continue at intervals through the night. She kept well above the rookery in passing. It was like a huge dark cage, hacked and sawn by great toothed beaks out of the heart of the forest. Intruders there were not viewed with favor by the sea-havals.

She was perhaps three hundred feet above the rookery and now well over toward the southern front of the forest when she came to an abrupt halt.

Throughout these hours her senses had been keyed to a pitch which automatically slapped a danger label on anything which did not match normal patterns of the overall forest scene. The outline which suddenly impressed itself on her vision was more than half blotted out by intervening thickets; but her mind linked the visible sections together in an instant. The composite image was that of a very large pale object.

And that was enough. She knew in the same moment that another tarm had been brought to the island by the Parahuans.

Nile stood where she was, frozen with dismay. There was no immediate cover available here; the slightest motion might bring her to the tarm's attention. The massive latticework of the forest was fairly open, with only scattered secondary growth between her and the clusters of thickets along the great slanted branch where the giant thing lay. The wild otters had reported seeing two of the creatures when the Parahuans first arrived. This one must have been kept aboard the big headquarters ship since then; it had been taken back to the surface to be used against her, had approached the island through the open sea to the south—

What was it doing in the upper forest levels? . . . Had it already discovered her?

The answer to the first question came immediately. The wind carried the scent of all life passing through the area to the west and along the lagoon up to the tarm. It was lying in wait for an indication that the human enemy was approaching the big blockhouse. A defensive measure against the Tuvela . . . and it was possible that it had, in fact, made out her shape, approaching along the floatwood branches in the night gloom, but hadn't yet defined her as human because she didn't bring with her a human scent.

Nile took a slow step backward, then another and a third, keeping her eyes fixed on what she could see of the tarm. As she reached the first cluster of screening growth, the great body seemed to be hunching, shifting position. The bushes closed behind her. Now the tarm was out of sight

. . . and it was difficult to avoid the thought that it had waited only for that instant to come swinging cunningly through the floatwood in pursuit, grappling branches with its tentacle clusters, sliding along the thicker trunks. She ran in lightweight balance toward a huge central bole, rounded it quickly, clutching the gnarled surface with hands and grip-soles, hesitated on the far side, eyes searching the area below.

Forty feet down was a twisted branch, thickets near its far end. Nile pushed off, dropped, landed in moments, knees flexing, ran along the branch and threaded her way into the thickets. From cover, she looked back. Nothing stirred above or behind her. The tarm hadn't followed.

She moved on less hurriedly, stopped at last to consider what she could do. She was still stunned by the encounter. Scentlessness would have been no protection if she had come much closer to that lurking sea beast before she discovered it. And how could she get to the oilwood now? The tarm lay so near it that it seemed suicidal recklessness to approach the area again. She scanned mentally over the weapons the floatwood offered. There was nothing that could stop a great creature like that quickly enough to do her any good. The UW's beam would only enrage it.

She had an abrupt sense of defeat. The thing might very well lie there till morning, making it impossible to start the beacon which was to identify the island to Parrol. There *must* be something she could do to draw it away from its position.

Almost with the thought, a vast bellowing erupted about her, seeming to come from inches beneath her feet, jarring her tight-drawn nerves again. . . . Only a sea-haval from the rookery below.

Nile's breath caught.

Only a sea-haval? From the rookery below—

She went hurrying on down through the forest.

Presently she returned, retracing her former route. But now she gave every section of it careful study—glancing ahead and back, planning it out, not as a line of ascent but of a headlong descent to follow. When she came back along it, she would be moving as quickly as she could move, unable to afford a single misstep, a single moment of uncertainty about what to do, or which way to turn. A good part of that descent would be low-weight jumping; and whenever one of the prospective jumps looked at all tricky, she tried it out before climbing farther.

She reached a point at last where she must be within a minute of sighting the tarm . . . if it had stayed where it was. For it might have been having second thoughts about the upright shape which had been coming toward it and then backed away, and be prowling about for her now. Nile moved as warily and stealthily as she ever had in her life until she knew she was within view of the branch where the tarm had lain. She hadn't approached it from the previous direction but had climbed up instead along the far side of the great bole which supported most of the floatwood and other growth in the area.

When she edged around the bole, she saw the tarm immediately where she had judged it would be—flattened out on the branch, the head end of the big worm body turned toward her. A great lidless pale eye disk seemed fixed on the bole. Something thick and lumpy—the mass of retracted tentacles—stirred along the side. There was a deceptively sluggish heavy look about the thing.

Nile glanced back and down along her immediate line of retreat. Then she took the UW from its holster and stepped out on a branch jutting from the massive trunk. Weaving tips lifted abruptly from the tarm's clumped tentacles. Otherwise it didn't move. Nile pointed the gun at the center of the horny eye lens and held down the trigger.

The tarm's body rose up. Nile snapped the gun into the holster, slipped back around the bole. Turned and sprang.

There was a sound of something like tons of wet sand smashing against the far side of the bole as she darted through a thicket thirty feet down. She swung out below the thicket, dropped ten feet, dropped twenty-five feet, dropped again, descending a stairway of air. . . .

A deep howling swept by overhead, more like the voice of the storm than that of an animal. Nile turned, saw the tarm, contracted almost to the shape of a ball, hurtle through smashing growth a hundred feet above, suspended from bunched thick tentacles. She pulled out the UW and held the beam centered on the bulk, shouting at the top of her lungs. The awesome cry cut off and the big body jerked to a stop, hung twisting in midair for an instant, attached by its tentacles to fifty points of the floatwood. Then the tarm had located her and swiftly came down. Nile slipped behind a trunk, resumed her retreat.

She was in and out of the tarm's sight from moment to moment, but the next series of zigzagging downward leaps did not draw her away from it again. She heard its crashing descent, above and to this side or that, always following, cutting down distance between them—then stench and noise exploded about. Strain blurred her vision, but there was a wide opening among the branches below and she darted toward it. A horizontal branch came underfoot—a swaying narrow bridge, open space all about and beneath. Sea-haval stink roiled the air. Heavy stirrings below, angry rumble. . . .

A great thump behind her. The branch shook violently. The tarm's howl swelled at her back, and furious bellowings replied. The branch creaked. Ahead to the right were the waving thickets she remembered—

Nile flung herself headlong off the branch into the growth, clutching with arms and legs. An explosively loud crack, not yards away—another. Then, moments later, a great thudding splash below.

Then many more sounds. Rather ghastly ones. . . .

Nile scrambled farther into the thicket, found solid foothold and stood up, gripping the shrubbery. She fought for breath, heart pounding like an engine. The racket below began to settle into a heavy irregular thumping as the beaks of the sea-havals slammed again and again into the rubbery monster which had dropped into their rookery, gripping a branch of floatwood . . . a branch previously almost cut through at either end by the beam of Nile's gun. The tarm was finished; the giant kesters wouldn't stop until it had been tugged and ripped apart, tossed in sections about the evil-smelling rookery, mashed to mud under huge webbed feet.

Nerves and lungs steadying gradually, Nile wiped sweat from her eyes and forehead, then looked over her gear to make sure nothing of importance had been lost in that plunging chase. All items seemed to be on hand.

And now, unless she ran into further unforeseen obstacles on the way, she should be able to get her oilwood fire started. . . .

There were no further obstacles.

For the fourth or fifth time Nile suddenly came awake, roused perhaps by nothing more than a change in the note of the wind. She looked about quickly. A dozen feet below her, near the waterline, an otter lifted its oval head, glanced up. It was the wild female, taking her turn to rest while her mate and Sweeting patrolled.

"Is nothing, Nile . . ." The otter yawned, dropped her head back on her forelegs.

Nile turned her wrist, looked at her watch. Still about two hours till dawn. . . . She'd been dozing uneasily for around the same length of time at the sea edge of the forest, waiting for indications of Parrol's arrival. Current conditions on the island had the appearance of a stalemate of sorts. On the surface, little happened. The Parahuans had withdrawn into their installations. An occasional boat still moved cautiously about the lagoon, but those on board weren't looking for her. If anything, since the last developments, they'd seemed anxious to avoid renewed encounters with the Tuvela. There was underwater activity which appeared to be centered about the ship beneath the lagoon floor. If she'd had a jet rig, she would have gone down to investigate. But at present the ship was out of her reach; and while the otters could operate comfortably at that depth, their reports remained inconclusive.

In spite of the apparent lull, this remained an explosive situation. And as she calculated it, the blowup wouldn't be delayed much longer. . . .

It must seem to the Voice of Action that it had maneuvered itself into an impossible situation. To avoid the defeat of its policies, it had, by its own standards, committed a monstrous crime and dangerously weakened the expeditionary force's command structure. Porad Anz would condone the slaughter of the opposed Great Palachs and Palachs only if the policies could be successfully implemented.

And now, by the Voice of Action's own standards again, the policies already had failed completely to meet the initial test. The basis of their argument had been that Tuvelas could be defeated. Her death was to prove it. With the proof at hand, the fact at last established, the attack on the planet would follow.

Hours later, she not only was still alive but was in effect disputing their control of the upper island areas. They must have armament around which could vaporize not only the island but the entire floatwood drift and her along with it. But while they remained here themselves, they couldn't employ that kind of armament. They couldn't use it at all without alerting the planet—in which case they might as well begin the overall attack.

Their reasoning had become a trap. They hadn't been able to overcome one Tuvela. They couldn't expect then that an attack on the Tuvelas of the planet would result in anything but failure. But if they pulled out of Nandy-Cline without fighting, their crime remained unexpiated, unjustified—unforgivable in the eyes of Porad Anz.

Nile thought the decision eventually must be to attack. Understaffed or not, their confidence shaken or not, the Voice of Action really no longer had a choice. It was simply a question now of when they would come to that conclusion and take action on it.

There was nothing she could do about that at present. At least she'd kept them stalled through most of the night; and if the Sotira racer had caught her warning, the planet might be growing aware of the peril overhanging it. Nile sighed, shifted position, blinking out through the branches before her at the sea. Starshine gleamed on the surging water, blended with the ghostly light of the luminous weed beds. Cloud banks rolled through the sky again. Fitful flickering on the nearby surface was the reflection of the oilwood. If Parrol would only get here . . .

She slid back down into sleep.

Something very wet was nuzzling her energetically. She shoved at it in irritation. It came back.

"Nile, wake up! Spiff's here!"

Grogginess vanished instantly. "Huh? Where are—"

"Coming!" laughed Sweeting. "Coming! Not far!"

She'd picked up the tiny resonance in the caller receiver which told her Spiff was in the sea, within three miles, homing in on her. And if Spiff was coming, Parrol was with him. Limp with relief, Nile slipped down to the water's edge with the otter. Almost daybreak, light creeping into the sky behind cloud cover, the ocean black and steel-gray, great swells running before the island.

"Which way?"

Sweeting's nose swung about like a compass needle, held due south. She was shivering with excitement. "Close! Close! We wait?"

"We wait." Nile's voice was shaky. "They'll be here fast enough . . ." Parrol had done as she thought—read the oil wood message from afar, set his car down to the south, worked it in subsurface toward the floatwood front. He'd be out of it now with Spiff, coming in by jet rig and with equipment.

"Where are your friends? Has anything been happening?"

"Heh? Yes. Two ships under lagoon now. Big one."

"Two— Has the command ship moved up?"

"Not *that* big. Waddle-feet carrying in things."

"What kind of things?"

Sweeting snorted. "Waddle-feet things, heh? Maybe they leave. Ho! Spiff's here. . . ."

She whistled, went forward into the water. Nile stood watching intently. Against the flank of a great rising wave two hundred yards out, two otters appeared for an instant, were gone again. . . .

"You look something of a mess, Dr. Etland!"

She'd jerked half around on the first low-pitched word, had the gun out and pointing as his voice registered on her consciousness. She swore huskily. "Thought you were a—forget it!"

On the surface twenty feet to her right, straddling the saddle of a torpedo-shaped carrier, Parrol shoved black jet rig goggles up on his forehead, reached for a spur of floatwood to hold his position. A UW rifle was in his right hand. He grinned briefly. "Dr. Cay?"

"All right for the moment," Nile said. She replaced her gun, hand shaking. "Did you run into trouble coming in?"

"None at all. The immediate area's clear?"

"At present."

Parrol had left the mainland in response to Nile's first call for help nine hours previously. Most of the interval he'd spent being batted around in heavy typhoon weather with a static-blocked communicator. He was within two hours of the island when he got a close-contact connection with sledman fleet units and heard for the first time that Dr. Etland meanwhile had got out another message. The Sotira racer had received her chopped-off report about Parahuans, carried it within range of other sleds. It was relayed through and around disturbance areas, eventually had reached the mainland and apparently was reaching sled fleet headquarters all about Nandy-Cline. Parrol's informants couldn't tell him what the overall effect of the warning had been; if anything, communication conditions had worsened in the meantime. But there seemed to be no question that by now the planet was thoroughly alerted.

They speculated briefly on the possibilities. There might or might not be Federation warships close enough to Nandy-Cline to take an immediate hand in the matter. The planet-based Federation forces weren't large. If they were drawn into defensive positions to cover key sections of the mainland, they wouldn't hamper the Parahuans much otherwise. The mainland police and the Citizens Alert Cooperative could put up a sizable fleet of patrol cars between them. They should be effective in ground and air encounters, but weren't designed to operate against heavily armed spacecraft. In general, while there were weapons enough around Nandy-Cline, relatively few were above the caliber required to solve personal and business problems.

"The sleds have unwrapped the old spaceguns again," said Nile. "They'll fight, now they know what they'll be fighting."

"No doubt," Parrol agreed. "But the Navy and Space Scouts are the only outfits around organized for *this* kind of thing. We don't know if they're available at present, or in what strength. If your web-footed acquaintances can knock out communications completely—"

"Evidently they can."

Parrol was silent a moment. "Could get very messy!" he remarked. "And in spite of their heavy stuff, you figure they're already half convinced they'll lose if they attack?"

"Going by their own brand of logic, they must be. But I don't think it will keep them from attacking."

Parrol grunted. "Well, let's talk with the otters again. . . ."

The wild otters had joined the group. They confirmed Sweeting's report of the arrival of a second ship beneath the lagoon. It was more than twice the size of the first, anchored directly behind it. Parahuans were active about both. Parrol and Nile asked further questions and the picture grew clear. The second ship seemed to be a cargo carrier, and the Parahuans apparently were engaged in dismantling at least part of the equipment of their floatwood installations and storing it in the carrier.

"So they're clearing the decks," Parrol said. "And not yet quite ready to move. Now, if at this stage we could give them the impression that the planet *was* ready—in fact, was launching an attack on them—"

Nile had thought of it. "How?" she asked. "It would have to be a drastic demonstration now. Not blowing up their blockhouse. Say something like hitting the command ship."

"We can't reach that. But we can reach the two under the lagoon. And we can get rather drastic about them."

"With what?"

"Implosion bombs," Parrol said. "Your message suggested I should bring the works, so I did. Three Zell-Eleven two pounders, tactical, adherent." He nodded at the equipment carrier in the water below them. "In there with the rest of it."

"Their ship locks are open," said Nile, after a moment. "Two should do it. One in each lock."

"Spaceships. It may not finish them. But—"

They glanced over at Spiff. He'd been watching them silently, along with the other three.

"Like to do a little bomb hauling again, Spiff?" Parrol inquired.

The big otter's eyes glistened. He snorted. Parrol got to his feet.

"Brought your rig," he told Nile. "Let's go pick up Dr. Cay and get him out to the car. He'll be safest there. Then we'll take a look at those ships. . . ."

Trailing Parrol and the carrier out to the aircar, Nile darted along twenty feet below the surface, the twin to his UW rifle clasped against her, luxuriating in the jet rig's speed and maneuverability. They'd left the otters near the floatwood; fast as they were, Sweeting and her companions couldn't have maintained this pace. It was like skimming through air. The rig's projected field nearly cancelled water friction and pressure; the rig goggles clamped over Nile's eyes pushed visibility out a good two hundred yards, dissolving murk and gloom into apparent transparency. Near the surface, she was now the equal of any sea creature in its own element. Only the true deeps remained barred to the jet rig swimmer. The Parahuan rigs she'd seen had been relatively primitive contrivances.

Parrol, riding the carrier with Ticos Cay asleep inside, was manipulating the vehicle with almost equal ease. It too had a frictionless field. He slowed down only in passing through the denser weed beds. By the time they reached the aircar, riding at sea anchor in the center of a floating thicket, a blood-red sun rim had edged above the horizon.

They got Ticos transferred to the car, stowed the carrier away, locked the car again, made it a subsurface race back to the floatwood and gathered up the otters. Spiff and Sweeting knew about tactical bombs by direct experience; their wild cousins knew about human explosives only by otter gossip and were decidedly interested in the operation. Roles were distributed and the party set off. Spiff, nine foot bundle of supple muscle, speed, and cold nerve, carried two of Parrol's implosion devices strapped to his chest in their containers. He'd acted as underwater demolition agent before. Parrol retained the third bomb.

And shortly Nile was floating in a cave of the giant roots which formed the island floor, watching the open locks of the two Parahuan spaceships below. A fog of yellow light spilled from them. Two points of bright electric blue hovered above the smaller ship, lights set in the noses of two midget boats turning restlessly this way and that as if maintaining a continuous scan of the area. There were other indications of general uneasiness. A group of jet-rigged Oganoon, carrying the heavy guns with which she had become familiar, floated between the sentry boats; and in each of the locks a pair of guards held weapons ready for immediate use.

All other activities centered about the lock of the larger ship. Parahuans manipulating packaged and crated items were moving into it from the sea in escorted groups, emerging again to jet off for more. Like the guards, they carried guide lights fastened to their heads.

Nile glanced around as Spiff came sliding down out of the root tangles above. The otters had returned to the surface to saturate themselves with oxygen before the action began. Spiff checked beside her, peering out through the roots at the ships, then tilted his head at her inquiringly. His depth-dark vision wasn't equal to hers but good enough for practical work. Nile switched on her rig speaker. "Dan?"

"I read you."

"Spiff's back and ready to go."

"My group's also on hand," Parrol's voice told her. "We'll start the diversionary action. Sixty seconds, or any time thereafter—"

Nile's muscles tightened. She gave Spiff a nod, watched him start off among the roots. Resting the barrel of the UW rifle on the root section before her, she glanced back and forth about the area below. Her position placed her midway between the two ship locks; Spiff was shifting to the right, to a point above the lock of the cargo carrier, his first target. Where Parrol and the other three otters were at the moment she didn't know.

A group of Oganoon approached the cargo lock again, guiding a burdened transport carrier. As they moved into the lighted area, the one in the lead leaped sideways and rolled over in the water, thrashing violently. The next in line drifted limply upward, long legs dangling. The ripping sound of Parrol's UW reached Nile's audio pickup a moment later.

There was abrupt milling confusion around and within the lock. The rest of the transport crew was struggling to get inside past the guards. Thumping noises indicated that a number of Parahuan weapons had gone off. A medley of watery voice sounds filled the pickup. Then one of the little boats was suddenly in purposeful motion, darting at a slant up from the ships toward the root floor of the island. The other followed.

"Boats have a fix on you and are coming, Dan!"

"I'm retreating."

The boats reached the roots, edged in among them. The

patrol above the smaller ship had dispersed, was now re-
grouping. Somebody down there evidently was issuing orders. Nile waited, heart hammering. Parrol's rifle snarled,
drew a heavier response, snarled again. Among the roots he
had a vast advantage in mobility over the boats. A swarm
of armed Parahuans jetted out from the smaller ship's lock.
One of them shifted aside, beckoned imperiously to the
patrol above. They fell in line and the whole group moved
quickly up to the roots. Their commanding officer dropped
back into the lock, stood gazing after them.

"The infantry's getting into the act," Nile reported.

"Leaving the ships clear?"

"Clear enough."

The transport crew had vanished inside the carrier. Its
two guards floated in the lock, shifting their weapons about.
The pair on duty in the other lock must still be there, but at
the moment only the officer was in sight. Nile studied him.
Small size, slight build—a Palach. He might be in charge
of the local operation. . . . Parrol's voice said, "I've given
the otters the go-ahead. They're hitting the infantry. Move
any time!"

Nile didn't answer. She slid the rifle barrel forward,
sighted on one of the carrier guards, locked down the trigger, swung to the second guard as the first one began a
back somersault. In the same instant she saw Spiff, half the
distance to the carrier already behind him, doubling and
thrusting as he drove down in a hunting otter's awesomely
accelerating sprint. He'd picked up his cue.

Now the Palach at the smaller ship floated in the rifle's
sights, unaware of events at the carrier. Nile held fire, tin-
gling with impatience. The two guards there hadn't showed
again; she wanted them out of the way before Spiff arrived.

The Palach glanced around, started back into the lock. She picked him off with a squeeze of her finger—and something dark curved down over the hull of the ship, flicked past the twisting body and disappeared in the lock.

Nile swallowed hard, slipped forward and down out of the cover of the roots. There were thumping sounds in the pickup; she couldn't tell whether some of them came now from the ship. Her mind was counting off seconds. Parrol's voice said something, and a moment later she realized she hadn't understood him at all. She hung in the water, eyes fixed on the lock entrance. Spiff might have decided his second implosion bomb would produce a better effect if carried on into the spaceship's guts—

A Parahuan tumbled out of the lock. Nile's hand jerked on the rifle, but she didn't fire. *That* Parahuan was dead! Another one. . . .

A weaving streak emerged from the lock, rocked the turning bodies in its passage, seemed in the same instant a hundred feet away in the water, two hundred—

Nile said shakily, "Bombs set, Dan! *Jet off!*"

She swung about, thumbed the rig's control grip, held it down, became a glassy phantom rushing through the dimness in Spiff's wake.

Lunatic beast—

Presently the sea made two vast slapping sounds behind them.

There was light at the surface now. Sun dazzle shifted on the lifting waves between the weed beds. The front of the floatwood island loomed a quarter of a mile to the north. Flocks of kesters circled and dipped above it, frightened into the upper air by the implosions which had torn out a central chunk of the lagoon floor.

"Can you see me?" Parrol's voice asked.

"Negative, Dan!" Nile had shoved the rig goggles up on her head. Air sounds rolled and roared about her. "Too much weed drift! I can't get far enough away from it for a clear look around."

"Same difficulty here. We can't be too far apart."

"Nobody seems to be trailing us," Nile said. "Let's keep moving south and clear this jungle before we try to get together."

Parrol agreed and she submerged again. Spiff and Sweeting were around, though not in view at the moment. The wild otters had stayed with Parrol. There was no real reason to expect pursuit; the little gunboats might have been able to keep up with them, but the probability was that they'd been knocked out among the roots by the bombs. She went low to get under the weed tangles, gave the otter caller a twist, glanced at her rig compass and started south. Parrol had a fix on the aircar. She didn't; but he'd said it lay almost due south of them now.

Sweeting and Spiff showed up half a minute later, assumed positions to her right and left . . . then there was a sound in the sea, a vague dim rumbling.

"You getting that, Nile?"

"Yes. Engine vibrations?"

"Should be something of that order. But it isn't exactly like anything I've ever heard. Any impression of direction?"

"No." She was watching the otters. Their heads were turning about in quick darting motions. "Sweeting and Spiff can't tell where it's coming from either. . . ." She added, "It seems to be fading at the moment."

"Fading here too," Parrol said. "Let's keep moving."

They maintained silence for a minute or two. The matted canopy of weeds still hung overhead. The strange sound became almost inaudible, then slowly swelled, grew stronger than before. There was a sensation as if the whole sea were shuddering faintly and steadily about her. She thought of the great spaceship which had been stationed in the depths below the floatwood drift these months. If they were warming up its drives, it might account for such a sound.

"Nile," Parrol's voice said.

"Yes?"

"Proceed with some caution! Our wild friends just showed up again. They indicate they have something significant to report. I'm shifting to the surface with them to hear what it is."

"All right," said Nile. "We'll stay awake."

She moved on, holding rig speed down to her companions' best traveling rate. The dim sea thunder about them didn't seem to change. She was about to address Parrol when his voice came again.

"Got the report," he said. "There's a sizable submersible moving about the area. Evidently it is *not* the source of the racket we're hearing. It's not nearly large enough for that. The otters have seen it three times—twice in deeper water, the third time not far from the surface. It was headed in a different direction each time. It may not be interested in us, but I get the impression it's quartering this section. That seems too much of a coincidence."

Nile silently agreed. She said, "Their detectors are much more likely to pick up your car than us."

"Exactly."

"What do we do, Dan?"

"Try to get to the car before the sub does. You hold the line south, keep near cover if you can. Apparently I'm somewhere ahead of you and, at the moment, closer to the sub. The otters are out looking for it again. If we spot it on the way to the car, I'll tag it."

"Tag it?"

"With bomb number three," Parrol said. "Had a feeling it might be useful before we were through. . . ."

Nile gave Spiff and Sweeting the alert sign, indicating the area before them. They pulled farther away on either side, shifted to points some thirty feet ahead of her. Trailing weed curtains began limiting visibility and the overhead blanket looked as dense as ever. The rumbling seemed louder again, a growing irritation to tight nerves. . . . Then soggy tendrils of vegetation suddenly were all about. Nile checked rig speed, cursing silently, pulled and thrust through the thicket with hands and feet. And stopped as she met Sweeting coming back.

Something ahead. . . . She followed the otter down through the thicket to the edge of open water. Other drift thickets in the middle distance. Sweeting's nose pointed. Nile watched. For an instant then, she saw the long shadow outline of a submersible glide past below. Her breath caught. She cut in the rig, came spurting out of the growth, drove after the ship—

"Dan!"

"Yes?"

"If you see that sub, *don't* try to tag it!"

"Why not?"

"Because it's *ours*, idiot! I was looking down on it just now. It's a Narcotics Control boat! And at a guess the reason it's been beating around here is that it has its detectors locked on the Parahuan command ship—"

The receiver made a muffled sound of surprise. Then, quickly: "It's probably not alone!"

"Probably not. How far do you register from your car?"

"Nine hundred yards," Parrol's voice said. "By the time we get together and make it there, we might—"

"We might be in the middle of a hot operation!"

"Yes. Let's get back upstairs and see what we can see."

Nile jetted up through the water, trailed by darting otter shapes, broke surface in a surging tangle of drift growth, began splashing and crawling out of the mess. Morning sun blazed through wind-whipped reeds about and above her.

"Nile," snapped the intercom, "their ship's here!"

"*Their* ship?"

"It's got to be the Parahuan. Something beneath me— lifting! Looks like the bottom of the ocean coming up. Keep out of the way—that thing is *big!* I'm scrambling at speed."

The intercom went silent. Nile stumbled across a pocket of water, lunged through a last tangle of rubbery brown growth, found open sea before her. The drift was rising sluggishly on a great swell. She shoved the goggles up on her head. Something shrieked briefly above. An aircar swept past, was racing back into the sky. Higher up, specks glinted momentarily, circling in the sun. A chain of patrol cars, lifting toward space, cutting through the aliens' communication blocks—

The swell had surged past; the weed bed was dropping toward its trough, shut off by a sloping wall of water to the south. Nile knifed into the sea, cut in the rig, swept upward, reached and rode the shifting front of the wave. View unobstructed.

"Sleds coming, Dan! Three of them."

His voice said something she didn't catch. Off to the right, less than half a mile away, the black hull of the Parahuan command ship lifted glistening from the sea. Rounded back of a giant sea beast. Nile tried to speak again and couldn't. Wind roar and sea thunder rolled about her. Out of the west, knifing lightly through the waves like creatures of air, the three sleds came racing in line on their cannon drives. On the foredeck of the one in the lead, the massive ugly snouts of spaceguns swiveled toward the Parahuan ship, already a third clear of the water and rising steadily. Pale beams winked into existence between the sled's guns and the ship, changed to spouts of smashing green fire where they touched the dark hull. The following sleds swung left, curving in; there were spaceguns there too, and the guns were in action. About the spaceship the ocean exploded in steam. Green fire glared through it. A ragged, continuous thundering rolled over Nile. The ship kept lifting. The sleds' beams clung. There was no return fire. Perhaps the first lash of the beams had sealed the ship's gunports. It surged heavily clear of the sea, fled straight up into the sky with an enormous howling, steam and water cascading back from it. The beams lifted with it, then winked out in turn, ceasing their thunder.

Nile's ears still rang with the din. Lying back in the water, she watched the ship dwindle in a brilliant blue sky.

Run, Palachs, run! But see, it's too late!

Two thin fire lines converged in the blue on the shrinking dot of the Parahuan ship. Then a new sun blazed in white fury where the dot had been. The fire lines curved away, vanished.

Federation warships had come hunting out of space. . . .

She swung about in the water, saw a section of a broken floatwood bough twenty feet away, caught it and clambered aboard. A wave lifted the bough as she came to her feet, sent it rushing south. Nile rode it, balanced against a spur, gaze sweeping the sea . . . a world of brilliance, of dazzling flashes, of racing wind and tumbling whitecaps. Laughter began to surge in her, a bubbling release. One of the great sleds knifed past, not a hundred yards away, rushing on humming drives toward the island. A formation of CA patrol cars swept above it, ports open. Jet chutists would spill from the ports in minutes to start cleaning the abandoned children of Porad Anz from the floatwood.

Details might vary considerably. But as morning rolled around the world, this was the scene that was being repeated now wherever floatwood drifts rode the ocean currents. The human demon was awake and snarling on Nandy-Cline. . . .

"Nile—"

"Dan! Where are you?"

"On the surface. Just spotted you. Look southwest. The aircar's registering. Dr. Cay's all right. . . ."

Flick of guilt—*I forgot all about Ticos!* Her eyes searched, halted on a swell. There he was.

She flung up an arm and waved, saw Parrol return the salute. Then she cut in the rig, dived from the floatwood, went down and flashed through the quivering crystal halls of the upper sea to meet him.

10

"You ARE *not*," said the blonde emphatically, "Dr. Ticos Cay. You are *not* Dr. Nile Etland. There are *no* great white decayed-looking monsters chasing you through a forest!"

Rion Gilennic blinked at her. She was an attractive young creature in her silver-blue uniform; but she seemed badly worried.

"No," he told her reassuringly. "Of course not."

The blonde brightened. "That's better! Now, who are you? I'll tell you who you are. You're Federation Council Deputy Rion Gilennic."

"Quite right," Gilennic agreed.

"And where are you?"

He glanced about. "In the transmitter room."

"Anybody can see that. Where's this transmitter room?"

"On the flagship. Section Admiral Tatlaw's flagship. Oh, don't worry! When I'm myself, I remember everything. It's just that I seem to slide off now and then into being one of the other two."

"You told us," the blonde said reproachfully, "that you'd absorbed recall transcriber digests like that before!"

"So I have. I realize now they were relatively minor digests. Small doses."

She shook her head. "This was no small dose! A double dose, for one thing. A twenty-six minute bit, and a two minute bit. Both loaded with emotion peaks. Then there was a sex crossover on the two minute bit. That's confusing in itself. I think you've been rather lucky, Deputy! Next time you try out an unfamiliar psych machine, at least give the operators straight information. On a rush job like this we had to take some things for granted. You *could* have stayed mixed up for weeks!"

"My apologies," said Gilennic. Then he made a startled exclamation.

"Now what?" the blonde asked anxiously.

"What time is it?"

She checked her watch. "Ship or standard?"

"Standard."

She told him. Gilennic said, "That leaves me something like ten minutes to get straightened out before Councilman Mavig contacts me."

"I can give you a shot that will straighten you out in thirty seconds," the blonde offered.

"Then I won't remember the digests."

"No, not entirely. But you should still have the general idea."

Gilennic shook his head. "That's not good enough! I need all the details for the conference."

"Well, I understand the Councilman's absorbed the digests too. He may not be in any better shape."

"That'll be the day!" said Gilennic sourly. "Nothing shakes the Councilman."

She reflected, said, "You'll be all right, I think. You've been coming out of it fast. . . . Those two subjects had some remarkable experiences, didn't they?"

"Yes, remarkable. Where are they at present?"

She looked concerned again. "Don't you remember? They left ship almost an hour ago. On your order. Dr. Etland wanted to get Dr. Cay back to the planet and into a hospital."

Gilennic considered. "Yes, I do remember now. That was just before this stuff began to take effect on me, wasn't it? I suppose—"

He broke off as the entrance door slid open. A trim young woman stepped in, smiled, went to the transmitter stand, placed a sheaf of papers on it, and switched on the screen. She glanced about the other items on the stand and looked satisfied.

"These are the reports you wanted for the conference, Mr. Gilennic," she announced. "You'll have just time enough to check them over."

"Thanks, Wyl." Gilennic started for the stand.

"Anything else?" Wyl asked.

"No," he said. "That will be all."

Wyl looked at the blonde. "We'd better be leaving."

The blonde frowned. "The Deputy isn't in good condition!" she stated. "As a Psychology Service technician, I have a Class Five clearance. Perhaps—"

Wyl took her arm. "Come along, dear. I'm Mr. Gilennic's confidential secretary and have a Class Two clearance. That isn't good enough to let me sit here and listen."

The blonde addressed Gilennic. "If you start running hallucinations again—"

He smiled at her. "If I do, I'll buzz for help. Good enough?"

She hesitated. "If you don't put it off too long, it will be. I'll wait beside the buzzer." She left the room with Wyl, and the door slid shut.

Rion Gilennic sighed and sat down at the stand. His brain felt packed—that was perhaps the best way to describe it. Two sets of memories that weren't his own had been fed in there in the time span of fifty seconds. He gathered that the emotional effects they contained were damped out as far as possible; but they remained extraordinarily vivid memories as experienced by two different sensory patterns and recorded by two different and very keen minds. For the next several hours, a part of him would be in effect Dr. Ticos Cay, able to recall everything that had occurred from his first realization of a search party of alien beings closing in stealthily on the floatwood hideout to the moment consciousness drained from him in the incubator pod. And another part would be Dr. Nile Etland, scanning at will over the period between her discussion with the Sotira sledmen and her return to the mainland with Danrich Parrol, Dr. Cay, and a pair of mutant otters.

By now Gilennic's mind seemed able to recognize these implants for what they were and to keep them distinct from his personal memories. But for a while there'd been confusion and he'd found himself running colorful floatwood nightmares in a wide-awake condition, blanked out momentarily on the fact that he was not whichever of the two had experienced that particular sequence. He'd really been much less upset about it than the two transcriber technicians who evidently blamed themselves for the side-effects. A recall digest, in any case, was the fastest and most dependable method known to get *all* pertinent information on a given set of events from a person who'd lived through them; and a few hours from now the direct impressions would fade from his mind again. No problem there, he decided. . . .

He flicked through the reports Wyl had left. Among them was one from the surgeon's office on the condition of Dr. Ticos Cay—a favorable prognosis. In spite of his age Dr. Cay's recuperative ability remained abnormally high. He'd been near total exhaustion but should recover in a few weeks of treatment. Gilennic was glad to see the memo; he'd been worried about the old man.

The latest report on military developments had nothing of significance. Most of the fighting had been concluded five hours ago, almost before the Etland party reached the mainland. Space pursuit continued; but the number of targets was down to twelve. Gilennic considered. Call Tatlaw and tell him to let a few more get away? No, two shiploads were enough to carry the bad word to Porad Anz. Too many lucky escapees would look suspicious—the Parahuans had learned the hard way that Fed ships could run them down. Some eight hundred Oganoon, holed up in a floatwood island, had been taken alive. The Palachs with them were dead by suicide. No value to that catch—

The other reports weren't important. The Psychology Service was doctoring newscast sources on Nandy-Cline. He'd hear more about that in the conference.

Gilennic sat a moment reflecting, smiled briefly. Not a bad setup, he thought. Not bad at all!

"Ship's comm section to Deputy Gilennic," said the screen speaker.

"Go ahead," he told it.

"Transmission carrier now hot and steady, sir! Orado is about to come in. When I switch off, the transmission room will be security-shielded."

"Double check the shielding," Gilennic said and pushed down the screen's ON button.

"What decided you to give the order to allow two Parahuan warships to escape?" Federation Councilman Mavig asked.

Gilennic looked at the two men in the screen. With Mavig

was Tolm Sindhis, a Psychology Service director—publicity angles already were very much a part of the situation, as he'd expected. The discussion wasn't limited to the three of them; Mavig had said others were attending on various extensions on the Orado side. He hadn't given their names and didn't need to. Top department heads were judging the Federation Council Deputy's actions at Nandy-Cline. Very well. . . .

Gilennic said, "Section Admiral Tatlaw's fleet detachment was still approaching the system when we picked up a garbled report from Nandy-Cline indicating the fighting had started there. Tatlaw went in at speed. By the time the main body of the detachment arrived, Parahuan ships were boiling out into space by twos and threes. Our ships split up and began picking them off.

"It was clear that something drastic had happened to the enemy on the planet. The colonial forces were in action, but that couldn't begin to account for it. The enemy wasn't in orderly retreat—he was breaking from the planet in absolute panic. Whatever the disaster was, I felt it was likely to be to our advantage if Porad Anz were permitted to receive a first-hand account of it by informed survivors.

"The flagship had engaged the two largest Parahuan ships reported so far, approximately in our cruiser class. It was reasonable to assume they had high-ranking Parahuans on board. We know now that except for the headquarters ship, which was destroyed before it could escape from the planet's atmosphere, they were in fact the two largest ships of the invasion. There was no time to check with Orado, even if it had been possible in the infernal communication conditions of the system. We were in a running fight, and Tatlaw would have cut the enemy apart in minutes. I was the leading representative of the civilian government with the detachment. Therefore I gave the order."

Mavig pursed his lips. "The Admiral didn't entirely approve of the move?"

"Naturally not," said Gilennic. "From a tactical point of view it made no sense. There were some moments afterward when I was inclined to doubt the wisdom of the move myself."

"I assume," Mavig said, "your doubts were resolved after you absorbed the digest of Dr. Etland's recall report."

"Yes. Entirely so."

Mavig grunted.

"Well, we know now what happened to the invasion force," he remarked. "Its command echelons were subjected to a concentrated dose of psychological warfare, in singularly appalling form. Your action is approved, Deputy. What brought Dr. Etland and her companions to your attention?"

"I went down to the planet at the first opportunity," Gilennic said. "There was still a great deal of confusion and I could get no immediate explanation for the Parahuan retreat. But I learned that a warning sent out by a Dr. Etland from one of the floatwood islands had set off the action. She reached the mainland at about that time, and I found her at the hospital to which she'd taken Dr. Cay. She told me in brief what had occurred, and I persuaded her to accompany me to the flagship with Dr. Cay. She agreed, on condition that Dr. Cay would remain under constant medical attention. She took him back to a mainland hospital a short while ago."

Mavig said, "The people who know about this—"

"Dr. Etland, Dr. Cay, Danrich Parrol," said Gilennic. "The

two recall transcriber technicians know enough to start thinking. So does my secretary."

"The personnel will be no problem. The other three will maintain secrecy?"

"They've agreed to it. I think we can depend on them. Their story will be that Dr. Etland and Dr. Cay discovered and spied on Parahuans from hiding but were not seen by them and had no contact with them. There'll be no mention made of the Tuvela Theory or of anything else that could be of significance here."

Mavig glanced at the Psychology Service director. Sindhis nodded, said, "Judging by the personality types revealed in the recall digests, I believe that's safe. I suggest we give those three people enough additional information to make it clear why secrecy is essential from the Federation's point of view."

"Very well," Mavig agreed. "It's been established by now that the four other water worlds which might have been infiltrated simultaneously by Parahuans are clear. The rumored enemy action was concentrated solely on Nandy-Cline. We're proceeding on that basis." He looked at Tolm Sindhis. "I understand your people have begun with the publicity cover work there?"

"Yes," Sindhis said. "It should be simple in this case. We're developing a popular local line."

"Which is?"

"That the civilian and military colonial forces beat the fight out of the invaders before they ever got back to space. It's already more than half accepted."

Gilennic said thoughtfully, "If it hadn't been for Dr. Etland's preparatory work, I'm inclined to believe that's what would have occurred. Not, of course, without very heavy human casualties. The counterattack certainly was executed with something like total enthusiasm."

"It's been a long time between wars," Mavig said. "That's part of our problem. How about the overall Hub reaction, Director?"

"We'll let it be a three day sensation," said Sindhis. "Then we'll release a series of canned sensations which should pretty well crowd the Nandy-Cline affair out of the newscasts and keep it out. I foresee no difficulties."

Mavig nodded. "The follow-up then. I rather like that term 'gromgorru.' We can borrow it as the key word here."

"Gromgorru and Tuvela-Guardians," said Tolm Sindhis.

"Yes. The two escaped cruisers reached Porad Anz. The sole survivors of the invasion present their story. The top echelons of the Everliving have a week or two to let new Tuvela-fear soak through their marrows. There is no word of a significant reaction in the Federation. What happens then? Deputy, you've shown commendable imagination. How would you suggest concluding the matter?"

"How would Tuvela-Guardians conclude it?" said Gilennic. "Dr. Etland set the pattern for us, I think. The attitude is not quite contempt, but not far from it. We've taken over a thousand low-grade prisoners for whom we have no use. Guardians don't kill purposelessly. In a week or two the prisoners should be transported to Porad Anz."

"By a fleet detachment?" Mavig asked.

Gilennic shook his head.

"One ship, Councilman. An impressive ship—I'd suggest a Giant Scout. But only one. The Guardian Etland came alone to the floatwood. By choice, as far as the Parahuans know. The Guardians would not send a fleet to Porad Anz. Or more than one Guardian."

"Yes—quite right. And then?"

"From what Dr. Cay was told," Gilennic said, "there are no surviving human captives on Porad Anz. But we'd make sure of that, and we'd let them know we're making sure of it. Half dead or insane, we don't leave our kind in enemy hands."

Tolm Sindhis said, "The Service will supply a dozen xenopaths to the expedition. They'll make sure of it."

Mavig nodded. "What else, Deputy?"

"Men were murdered on Nandy-Cline," said Gilennic. "The actual murderers are almost certainly dead. But the authorities on Porad Anz need a lesson—for that, and simply for the trouble they've made. They're territory-greedy. How about territorial restrictions?"

Mavig said, "Xeno intelligence indicates they've occupied between eighteen and twenty water planets. They can be told to evacuate two of those planets permanently—say the two closest to the Federation—and given a limited time in which to carry out the order. We'll be back presently to see it's been done. Would that sum it up?"

"I think," said Gilennic, "a Guardian would say so." He hesitated, added, "I believe the terms Tuvela or Guardian should not be used in this connection by us, or in fact used by us at all. The Everliving of Porad Anz can form their own conclusions about who it is that issues them orders in the name of the Federation. As far as we're concerned, the superhumans can fade back now into mystery and grom-gorru. They'll be more effective there."

Mavig nodded, glanced aside. "I see," he remarked, "that meanwhile the selection of the person who is to issue the Council's orders to Porad Anz has been made." He pressed a button on the stand before him. "Your transmission duplicator, Deputy—"

Rion Gilennic slid a receptacle from the stand duplicator, took a card from it, saw, without too much surprise, that the name on the card was his own. "I'm honored by the assignment," he said soberly.

"You can start preparing for it." Mavig shifted his gaze to Tolm Sindhis. "We should expect that some weeks from now there'll be individuals on Nandy-Cline taking a discreet interest in the backgrounds of Dr. Etland and Dr. Cay. It might be worth seeing what leads can be developed from them."

The director shrugged. "We'll watch for investigators, of course. My opinion is, however, that if the leads take us anywhere, they'll show us nothing new. . . ."

CONCLUSIONS OF THE EVALUATING COMMITTEE OF THE LORDS OF THE SESSEGUR, CHIEFS OF THE DARK SHIPS

SUBJECT: THE HUMAN-PARAHUAN ENGAGEMENT OF NANDY-CLINE

The committee met in the Purple Hall of the Lord Ildaan. Present besides the Lord Ildaan and the permanent members of the Committee were a Wirrollan delegation led by its Envoy Plenipotentiary. The Lord Ildaan introduced the Envoy and the members of the delegation to the Committee and referred to the frequently voiced demands of Wirrolla and its associated species that the Alliance of the Lords of the Sessegur should agree to coordinate and spearhead a unified attack on the Federation of the Hub. He explained that the conclusions to be expressed by the Committee might serve as a reply to such demands. He then requested the Lord Toshin, High Ambassador of the Alliance to the Federation of the Hub, to sum up intelligence reports compiled in the Federation following the Parahuan defeat.

The Lord Toshin: The overall impression left in the Federation by the attempted Parahuan conquest of the world of Nandy-Cline is that it was an event of almost no significance. In the relatively short period before I left Orado to confer in person with other members of this Committee, it appeared that the average Federation citizen had nearly forgotten such an attempt had been made and certainly would have found it difficult to recall much more than the fact. We must understand, of course, that this same average citizen in all likelihood never before had heard of the planet of Nandy-Cline. The sheer number of Federation worlds blurs their individual significance.

On Nandy-Cline itself the conflict with the Parahuans naturally has remained a topic of prime interest. While we may suspect that the bulk of the Parahuan force was destroyed in space by Federation military, the continental population takes most of the credit for its defeat. No opinions have been obtained from the sizable pelagic population known as sledmen, who appear to be secretive by habit and treat Federation news personnel and other investigators with such scant civility that few attempt to question them twice.

There has been no slightest public mention in the Federation of the Parahuan Tuvela Theory. The person referred to in the reports of Parahuan survivors to Porad Anz as "the Guardian Etland," and believed by them to be a member of a special class of humans known as Tuvelas, does exist. Her name is Dr. Etland and she is a native of Nandy-Cline. My office had a circumspect but very thorough investigation made of her activities and background. Most of you are familiar with the result. It indicates that Dr. Etland is very capable and highly intelligent, but in a normally human manner. She is a biochemist by training and profession, and there is nothing to suggest overtly that she might be one of a group of perhaps mutated humans who have made themselves the secret rulers and protectors of the Federation. A simultaneous investigation made of her associate, Dr. Ticos Cay, believed by the Parahuans to be possibly another Tuvela, had similar results. We have no reason to think that Dr. Cay is more or other than he appears to be.

Of particular interest is the fact that there is no public knowledge in the Federation of the role ascribed to these individuals by Parahuan survivors in bringing about the evidently panic-stricken retreat from Nandy-Cline. On the planet Dr. Etland and Dr. Cay are generally credited with having given the first warning of the presence of alien intruders, but it is assumed that this is all they did.

Under the circumstances, I felt it would be unwise to attempt to have Dr. Etland questioned directly. It would have been impossible in any case to question Dr. Cay. After a period of hospitalization, he appears to have returned to his research on one of the many floating jungles of that world; and it is believed that only Dr. Etland is aware of his current whereabouts.

The Lord Ildaan: The Lord Mingolm, recently the Alliance's Ambassador to Porad Anz, will comment on discrepancies between the Federation's publicized version of the Parahuan defeat and the account given by Parahuan survivors.

The Lord Mingolm: As the Committee knows, only two of the Parahuan invasion ships escaped destruction and eventually returned to Porad Anz. Aboard those ships were eighty-two Palachs and Great Palachs, twenty-eight of whom had been direct witnesses of the encounter between the Everliving and the female human referred to as the Guardian Etland.

All of these twenty-eight were members of the political faction known as the Voice of Action and under sentence of death for their complicity in the disastrous revolt of the faction on Nandy-Cline. All were questioned repeatedly, frequently under severe torture. I attended a number of the interrogations and on several occasions was permitted to question the subjects directly.

Their stories agreed on every significant point. Both Dr. Cay and Dr. Etland had stated openly that Dr. Etland was a Guardian of the Federation and that the designation of Tuvela applied to her. Such statements would not have convinced the Voice of Action, which had argued vehemently against the implications of the Tuvela Theory in the past, and particularly against the claim that Tuvelas appeared to have supernormal powers. However, the chain of events which began with the arrival of Dr. Etland in the area where they were holding Dr. Cay did convince them. There seemed to be nothing they could do to check her. She came and went as she chose, whether in the sea or in the dense floating forests, and was traceless as a ghost. Moreover, those who had the misfortune of encountering her did not report the fact. They simply disappeared. The list of the missing included an advanced Great Palach, renowned as a deadly fighter and the leader of the Voice of Action, and two battle-trained tarms, which are most efficiently destructive giant beasts. When a majority of the Everliving voted to parley with the Guardian, she came voluntarily into their forest stronghold, spoke to them and ordered them off the planet. The Voice of Action realized the nerve of their colleagues had broken and that the order would be obeyed. In frenzy and despair they struck out at the yielding majority and gained control of the invasion forces.

But now the situation simply worsened. The Voice of Action had made its move under the assumption that the Guardian Etland, in her willingness to speak to the Everliving, had allowed herself to be trapped. At the time she was still in a guarded compartment of the stronghold, disarmed and in the company of Dr. Cay. But when a detachment was sent to execute her there, it was destroyed in a horribly vicious attack by native life forms which until then had appeared completely innocuous. Deadly fumes infested other sections of the fort; and there was so much confusion that considerable time elapsed before it was discovered that the Guardian had left the stronghold, evidently unharmed, and had taken Dr. Cay with her.

Neither of the two was seen thereafter, but there were continuing manifestations of the Guardian's presence in the area. The Great Palachs and Palachs of the Voice of Action, now in furious dispute among themselves as to what might be the best course to follow, retreated to the expedition's command ship and to two other space vessels in the vicinity. The ships were stationed at depths below the surface of the sea which seemed to place them beyond the reach of the Guardian, but presently the command ship received a fragmentary report that she was attacking the two other vessels. This was followed by violent explosions in which the two ships evidently were destroyed.

It was enough. The command ship broadcast an order to all divisions on Nandy-Cline to withdraw at once from the planet. As we know, this belated attempt to escape was not successful. The general human attack already had begun. The command ship apparently was annihilated in the planet's atmosphere, and in a short time the entire expeditionary force was virtually wiped out.

I must emphasize strongly the oppressively accumulating effect these events produced on the Parahuans during the relatively short period in which they occurred. As related by the survivors, there was a growing sense of shock and dismay, the conviction finally of having challenged something like an indestructible supernatural power. At the time they were questioned, the survivors still seemed more disturbed by this experience than by the practical fact of their own impending demise on orders of Porad Anz, of which they were aware. It is not only that at the end there were no Parahuan disbelievers in the Tuvela Theory on Nandy-Cline but that the Tuvelas seemed to have proved to be monstrously more dangerous even than had been assumed. The impression was strengthened by the fact that the Guardian Etland appeared to be a young female. The Parahuans are aware that in the human species as in many others it is the male who is by biological and psychic endowment as well as by tradition the fighter. What a fully mature male Tuvela might have done to them in the circumstances staggered their imagination. Evidently the Guardians had considered it unnecessary to employ one of their more formidable members to dispose of the invasion forces; and evidently their judgment was sound.

I must conclude that the account of the surviving Parahuan witnesses was objectively correct. What they reported did occur. The interpretation we should put on these events may be another matter. But the reports circulating in the Federation obviously were distorted in that the true cause of the Parahuan rout at Nandy-Cline—that is, the appearance and actions of Dr. Etland—was not made public. I offer no opinion on the possible reasons for the falsification.

The Lord Ildaan: The Lord Toshin will comment.

The Lord Toshin: I agree with the Lord Mingolm's conclusion. We can assume that the Parahuan survivors told the truth as they knew it. We must ask, then, why the Federation's official version of the Parahuan defeat did not refer to the Tuvela Theory, why Dr. Etland's name was barely mentioned, and why she is credited only with having warned of the enemy presence.

The simplest explanation might seem to be that she is in fact, as she claimed and as Dr. Cay claimed, a Tuvela-Guardian. But that confronts us with the other question of why a Guardian should reveal her most secret identity and expose her group to the enemy. To that question there is no reasonable answer.

Further, I see no room in the structure of the Federation's Overgovernment for a class of hidden rulers. It is a multi-layered complex in which the Federation Council, though popularly regarded as the central seat of authority, frequently appears to be acting more as moderator among numerous powerful departments. That all these organizations, led by very capable beings, should be the unwitting tools and pawns of Tuvela-Guardians may not be impossible but is highly questionable.

Therefore, I say we should not accept the possibility that Dr. Etland is a Guardian as a satisfactory explanation. I ask the Lord Ildaan to poll the Committee.

The Lord Ildaan: I poll the Committee and the Committee agrees. The Lord Toshin will resume comment.

The Lord Toshin: The second possible explanation is that

Dr. Etland, while not a Guardian and not in the Parahuan sense a Tuvela, has paranormal abilities and employed them to terrorize the invasion force to the point of precipitate retreat. I refer to what is known as the Uld powers. To this, I can say only that there is nothing in her record or reputation to indicate she has such abilities. Beyond that, lacking sufficient information on the human use of Uld powers, I shall offer no opinion.

The Lord Ildaan: The Lord Gulhad will comment.

The Lord Gulhad: At one time I made an extensive investigation of this subject in the Federation. My purpose was to test a theory that the emergence of a species from its native world into space and the consequent impact of a wide variety of physical and psychic pressures leads eventually to a pronounced upsurge in its use of Uld powers. The human species, of course, has been in space for a very short time in biological terms. Because of the recent acute disturbances in its political history, I was unable to obtain confirmation of the theory. The available records are not sufficiently reliable.

However, I could establish that the humans of our day make use of Uld powers more extensively than most other intelligent species now known to us. Humans who do so are called *psis*. There is little popular interest in psis in the Federation, and there is considerable misinformation concerning them. It is possible that several branches of the Overgovernment are involved in psi activities, but I found no proof of it. It is also possible that the Federation has advanced the nonbiological harnessing of Uld powers to an extent considerably beyond what is generally known, and is therefore relatively indifferent to its usually less exact control by living minds.

The question is then whether Dr. Etland, either directly or with the aid of Uld devices, could have used Uld powers to produce the disconcerting manifestations reported to the Committee by the Lord Mingolm. Did she incite normally harmless lower life forms to attack the Parahuans? Did she make herself invisible and generally untraceable? Did she cause opponents to disappear, perhaps into the depths of the sea, into space—even into dimensions presently unknown to us? Did she madden the minds of the Voice of Action, forcing them into their disastrous revolt? Was the explosion of the two submerged ships which triggered the abrupt retreat brought on by a manipulation of Uld powers?

All this is possible. We know or suspect that human psis and other users of Uld have produced phenomena which parallel those I listed.

However, it is improbable. In part because there is no record that any one Uld user could employ the powers in so many dissimilar ways. Even if we assume that Dr. Cay was also an accomplished psi and that the two worked together, it remains improbable.

It is further improbable because we cannot say that Dr. Etland could have achieved what she did only through the use of Uld power. Considered individually, each reported event might have had a normal cause. And since the deliberate control of Uld to a significant extent remains exceedingly rare also among humans, its use should not be assumed when other explanations are available.

The Lord Ildaan: I poll the Committee and the Committee agrees. The Lord Toshin will comment.

The Lord Toshin: There remains, as the Lord Gulhad indicated, a third possibility. I find it perhaps more disquieting than the two we have considered. It is, of course, that Dr. Etland is precisely what she seems to be—an exceptionally capable human, but one with no abnormal qualities and no mysterious authority. Our investigation indicated that she is thoroughly familiar with the floating forests of her world and the life forms to be found there, is skilled with weapons and on a number of occasions has engaged successfully in combat with her kind. Dr. Cay was a Parahuan captive long enough to have gained detailed information on the Tuvela Theory. It is difficult to see how he could have transmitted this knowledge to Dr. Etland. But if we assume he found a way of doing it, it seems we should accept, as the most probable explanation of the events reported by the Parahuan survivors, that Dr. Etland used the information and her familiarity with the area and its tactical possibilities, along with physical competence and ordinary weapons, to demoralize and eventually rout the enemy.

Of course, we cannot prove this. And evidently that is precisely what the Federation's Overgovernment intends, in seeing to it that no mention was made of Dr. Etland's role or the Tuvela Theory in the accepted reports on the Parahuan invasion. Any investigators who were aware of the Parahuan version of the affair would know something was being concealed but could only speculate, and perhaps speculate uneasily, on what was concealed. For note that it is not of major significance which of the possibilities considered here contains the answer. To an enemy, the individual we know as Dr. Etland would be as deadly in one aspect as in another. We should regard the silence of the Federation's authorities on the point as a warning directed to those who might base their actions on too definite a conclusion—such as the one made by Porad Anz. It implies that a hostile intruder cannot know in what shape disaster may confront him among humans, that if he comes he will face the unexpected—perhaps the uncalculable.

The Lord Mingolm: Still, we must calculate. We have established only that Dr. Etland was a dangerous individual. What information does the Parahuan mistake give us about the species?

The Lord Toshin: It confirms that the species is extremely variable. The Parahuan evaluation was based on the study of a few thousand individuals, plucked secretly from space over a long period of time and tested to destruction. No doubt Porad Anz learned a great deal about these humans in the process. Its mistake was to generalize from what it learned and to calculate from the generalizations. To say that *the* human is thus and so is almost to lie automatically. The species, its practices and philosophies remain unpredictable. Individuals vary, and the species varies with circumstances. This instability seems a main source of its strength. We cannot judge it by what it is today or was yesterday. We do not know what it will be tomorrow. That is the cause of our concern.

The Lord Ildaan: It is, indeed, the cause of our concern. And it seems from what has been said that the human Overgovernment must be considered now as a prime factor. The Lord Batras will comment.

The Lord Batras: The function of the Overgovernment is strategy. In part its strategies are directed at the universe beyond the Federation. But that is a small part.

Regard the Federation as the object of an invader's plans. It covers a vast area of space. Its inhabited worlds appear almost lost among the far greater number of worlds which support no human life. Below the central level, its political organization seems tenuous. Federation military power is great but thinly spread.

The area of the Federation would thus appear open to limited conquests by a determined and well prepared foe. But we are aware that during many star periods every such attempted thrust has failed. We have seen more subtle plans to weaken and cripple the human civilization fail as completely, and we still do not know specifically why some of them failed. However, on the basis of what we have observed, we can say in general now that the Federation is a biological fortress armed by the nature of its species. The fortress may be easily penetrated. When this occurs, it turns into a complex of unpredictable but always deadly traps.

This being true, we must ask why the Overgovernment persists in acting in a manner which appears almost designed to conceal the strength of the Federation's position. We have seen that its policy is to treat hostile activities as being of no importance and that it provides no more information concerning them than it can avoid. We may assume it genuinely believes its present galactic neighbors do not constitute a serious military threat. However, the great restraint it shows in retaliating for planned attacks must have a further reason. In the latest instance, it has not even forced Porad Anz to disarm, as it easily could have done.

I believe we have amassed sufficient information at last to explain the matter. The Overgovernment's main concern is with its own populations. What plans it has for the species we do not know. As yet, that defies analysis. But we know what plans it does not have for the species and the means it employs to keep it from turning into directions regarded as undesirable.

Consider the creature again as the Lord Toshin described

it. Individuals vary in attitude and behavior, but the creature as a class is eminently dangerous. It is, of course, inherently aggressive. Before the structure of the Federation was forged, humans fought one another for many star periods throughout that area with a sustained fury rarely observed in other species. Since that time they have remained technically at peace. But the aggressive potential remains. It expresses itself now in many ways within the confines of the human culture.

I said that we know what the human Overgovernment does not want. It does not want its unstable, variable, dangerous species to develop a philosophy of space conquest from which it could gain nothing it does not already have, and through which it might return eventually to the periods of interhuman conflict which preceded the Federation. Possibly the Overgovernment is influenced by additional considerations in the matter. We do not know that. We do know that the human species is oriented at present to deal with other intelligent beings in a nonhostile manner. There are criminal exceptions to that rule—we and others have clashed with them. But those exceptions are regarded as criminals also by their kind.

This general attitude could change if the present humans of the Federation gained the impression they were being seriously challenged by outside enemies. So far, they have been given no reason to believe it. The Parahuan invasion was a serious challenge only in the minds of Porad Anz. We anticipated its failure but believed we could gain information from it—as we have done.

I submit to the Committee that we now have gained information enough. The Overgovernment has shown it is afraid of the effects continuing irritations of the kind might have on its species. We too should be wise enough to be afraid of such effects. If the Federation is launched on a pattern of retaliatory conquests, the pattern might well become an established habit. That is the real danger.

The Lord Ildaan: The Committee agrees. I speak then as the Lord Ildaan, representing the Alliance of the Lords of the Sessegur, Chiefs of the Dark Ships. I address the Wirrollan delegation and all those they represent. To the ends of the area through which the influence of the Alliance extends there will be no further hostile action prepared or planned against the human Federation. The Alliance forbids it, and the Dark Ships enforce our ruling as they have done in past star periods. Be warned!

The Committee concurs. The meeting is closed.